'powerful, solid characters. And though the potent Jamaican accents are initially unsettling the inflection soon adds to the atmosphere. A well paced, occasionally introverted, journey into the depths of the human condition.' *Steve Lee, Big Issue*

Thompson's seco [...] l detail as it is in intrigue ... th [...] f such strongly drawn character [...] ith middle age, ensure that Tho  ough energy to carry the reader through these quiet [...] lscapes'. *Victoria Segal, The Times*

'A sweetly melancholy book about loss and belonging ... Thompson draws you in by mesmerising you with his subtle and tender characterisation.' *SleazeNation*

'Beautifully plotted, and in his sensitive interest in social outsiders, Thompson crafts an emotional honesty from a subject others would sensationalise or exploit.' (*Metro*)

'Amiable and quiet-toned while managing to disturb and convince.' *Stephen Blanchard, Time Out*

For *Meet Me Under the Westway*

'Stephen Thompson's best book. Read it.' *Nik Cohn*

'A funny, evocative, authentic account of a struggling playwright's rise from obscurity to semi-obscurity. Brilliant.' *Joe Penhall*

Also by Stephen Thompson

Missing Joe

Meet Me Under the Westway

Toy Soldiers

No More Heroes

Stephen Thompson

JACARANDA

First published in this edition in Great Britain 2015 by
Jacaranda Books Art Music Ltd
5 Achilles Road
West Hampstead
London NW6 1DZ
www.jacarandabooksartmusic.co.uk

A CIP catalogue record for this book is available from
the British Library

ISBN: 978 1 909762 12 1
eISBN: 978 1 909762 13 8

Typeset by Head & Heart Publishing Services
www.headandheartpublishingservices.com

Printed and bound in Great Britain
by CPI Group (UK) Ltd, Croydon, CR0 4YY

For Vanessa.

This book is dedicated to the victims of 7/7....and the heroes.

Prologue

It was unusual for me to leave Theodore's so early in the morning, but that afternoon I was working back in Duddenham and didn't want to be late for my shift. At Kings Cross I got caught up in the rush hour crowd and was swept down the escalator towards the Circle Line. I reached the platform to find it thick with commuters, three or four lines deep. After missing a couple of trains due to overcrowding, I finally boarded one heading for Paddington. Barely able to move, I positioned myself near the entrance, thinking it would be quicker to get off at Paddington but as it turned out, it wasn't the best decision.

With each new stop, I was jostled both by the people getting off the train and the ones getting on. By the time we arrived at Edgware Road I was feeling hot and tetchy, and my mood wasn't improved when the train got held up. All the passengers were ready and waiting to leave but the doors remained opened for several minutes. We could breathe at least, and Edgware Road is above ground so at least we weren't stuck in a tunnel, but even so, as the delay grew longer, a few people started tutting and sighing and one or two leaned out the doorway to see what the problem was. I was expecting to hear an announcement about the cause of the delay, but none came.

While we waited, I became conscious of being observed, and turned slightly to my left to see the man I now know to be Mohammad Sidique Khan staring at me. He was sitting on a row of four seats, two in from the double doors. I remember him very clearly because, unlike the rest of us, he looked cool and unflustered, without so much as a hint of sweat on his face. He gave me a squinty-eyed stare but I had the impression he wasn't really looking at me, rather he was somehow looking through me. Eventually he glanced at his watch then started fidgeting with the backpack on his lap. It wouldn't be true to say he unnerved me, you get used to all sorts of people on the tube, but instinctively I moved a little further along the carriage.

At long last we heard the driver say, 'This train is now ready to depart. Please stand clear of the closing doors.' A tall white man in a crumpled grey suit who was standing in front of me said, "Bout bloody time.' The engine hissed and grumbled, the doors slid jerkily together and the train crawled away from the platform. It was only eight thirty in the morning, but as soon as the doors closed I felt the heat rising. We were in the second carriage so it wasn't long before the train entered the tunnel. The walls were lined with power cables and studded with lamps and there was a patch of daylight coming in from the open platform we'd just left. It was also very wide, with enough space for two trains, and high enough for me to see the soot-covered roof.

What I remember next was a hissing sound and out of the corner of my eye a white searing light. Just as I turned to get a better look at it, there was a moment of eerie silence followed by an almighty blast that blew me clean off my feet sending me crashing against the window opposite. I bounced off the window and landed on my stomach on the floor. The carriage immediately went dark and filled with dust and debris. For several seconds nothing happened, I saw no movement, heard nothing except the loud ringing in my ears. Convinced that everyone was dead except me, my survival instincts took over. Dust filled my nose and mouth. To avoid choking to death, I wriggled out of my jacket and tied it into a makeshift bandage around my face, which was stinging and caked with grit. I was thinking *I should stand up* when the moaning started, quickly followed by the haunting cries for help, and then, soon after that, the piercing, chilling screams.

As the dust began to settle, I noticed a man sitting on the floor next to me, slightly hunched over, his legs splayed out to the sides like a rag doll. He wasn't moving. His eyes were open but expressionless. An arm was missing and there was blood spurting from his wound. I jumped up. It didn't even occur to me that I might be injured. When I was on my feet I suddenly thought to check myself for signs of serious damage. Everything seemed to be working. All my bits were there but the ringing in my ears seemed to be getting louder, my eyes were streaming from all the dust and even with my makeshift mask I was coughing so hard I could barely breathe.

Above the screams a male voice shouted, 'For the love of God, shut up!' Instantly the screams died down. Strange, how one's person voice had immediately quietened the entire carriage. Now standing, I started looking around. It was dark, but the light coming from the carriage behind was enough for me to see the extent of the damage. There was broken glass and debris everywhere. Lumps of metal and electrical wires dangled from the mangled ceiling. The seat cushions were in shreds. I took a step and almost fell into a gaping crater in the floor, the chunky metal warped and blackened and folded in, slick with grease. The area immediately around it was littered with personal effects – credit cards, wallets, keys – and spattered with human entrails. People were trapped under huge pieces of metal, some of them with arms and legs missing, some with half their heads caved in, others with no heads at all.

Lodged in the crumpled window frame I saw a woman's severed arm, a watch still on the wrist. The double doors had been completely blown off and from where I stood I could see a man lying on the tracks below. He'd lost both his legs, from the knees down, but he was fully conscious, his eyes were open and he kept swivelling his head left and right, as if he was only temporarily incapacitated and was preparing to get up and walk away. I knew he was without hope and it seemed to bring me to my senses. I began looking for a way out. The door to the carriage in front had collapsed and couldn't be opened, but the one leading to the carriage behind was still intact and was actually ajar. A knot of people fighting each other to get through it caused a bottleneck. Those who couldn't get through the adjoining door eventually lost patience and started clambering down through the double doors, using their arms to lower themselves on to the track. I did the same.

Down on the tracks, people were jumping from the other

carriages and running back towards Edgware Road station and all at once I was hit by the horror of the situation. Many people were dead; others were dying in agony. I felt for them but at that moment I was mainly concerned for my own safety. I was about to take off when I saw the guy with the missing legs lying on the tracks and something happened to me. I just couldn't leave him there by himself. Several people had stopped to inspect him, and one woman had actually crouched down and held his hand before saying she was going off to get help. For some reason I asked him his name. He was called Stuart. I was no doctor but I didn't need to be to see the danger he was in. 'You'll bleed to death if we don't get your legs bandaged. We have to do it but it's gonna hurt. You understand?' He looked at me, like a helpless dog, and nodded.

I took off my shirt and started ripping it. I had zero first-aid knowledge and it showed. In my anxiety to cover the bloodied stumps, I became all thumbs and had real problems tying knots in the tourniquets. The blood was running so freely, it immediately soaked through the material and made it almost impossible to get a grip on it. I managed it, though. Surprisingly, Stuart never once cried out or even winced. I guess he was in shock. While I was tending to him, I saw a black man hurrying towards me wearing a high-vis jacket and a safety helmet and clutching a walkie-talkie. I thought he was someone from the emergency services but he turned out to be a London Underground employee. His name was Charles and I later found out he was from Ghana. He hadn't been in the job a year. He couldn't have been more helpful. He told me to leave Stuart with him and to make my way back to Edgware

Road. 'The tracks are not live so it's OK.' I hadn't even thought of the possibility of being electrocuted.

'Go!' Charles screamed, 'It is too dangerous here.'

'What the hell happened?'

'No idea. They are saying it might have been a bomb.'

'A bomb? You mean, as in a terrorist bomb?'

He waved me away. 'Why are you still here? Go now.'

I looked at Stuart. He seemed to be passing in and out of consciousness. Charles assured me that the emergency services were minutes away so I stood up and started heading down the tracks. As I was leaving, I noticed there were still people moving about in the bombed out carriage, which, from the outside, looked like a semi-crushed sardine tin. From the tracks it was difficult to see exactly what they were doing but I knew they must have been trying to help the injured. Using my arms, I clambered up through the blown out doors. Charles saw me and shouted for me to get down, warning that the carriage could ignite at any moment, but I ignored him.

I once heard a war veteran talking on the radio about what it was like to fight on the beaches in Normandy. He said it didn't take him very long to get used to the death and destruction. 'You quickly learn to ignore your surroundings, you concentrate on the job in hand.' That's how I felt when I went back into that carriage. I was now so focussed on helping people I hardly noticed the curdled blood or the decapitated corpses.

Towards the rear of the carriage, near the adjoining door that hadn't been damaged, two white men were standing over a young black girl who was stretched out across a section of seating that hadn't been ripped out. She was trapped under a metal beam. I was in such a haste to get over there I slipped on a piece of bloodied material and almost fell over. When I got there I could see that the beam, big and solid, had come away from overhead and it would take a lot of time and manpower, and possibly machinery, to remove it. Half of it was wedged in the window and the other half had gone right through the floor. The girl under it, who couldn't have been older than eighteen had been blown out of her clothes. She was naked except for her underwear and was barely breathing. The men standing over her introduced themselves as Ian and Ed. Ian was in his early thirties and had weedy arms and a beer gut. Ed was older, late forties, and more robust-looking. He had a slight cut over his left brow, which was dripping blood into his eye. We three were the only able-bodied survivors left. The others had all gone.

Looking around, I saw several other injured people in the carriage. They were either lying or sitting on the floor, amongst the rubble, in various stages of agony, and were either incapable or unwilling to move. Among them was an elderly white woman who had broken both her legs, a young white guy with severe lacerations to his face and hands and a young white girl with a huge make-shift bandage around her head that was soaked in blood. We could do nothing for them except offer reassurances that the paramedics were on their way.

I turned my attention to the girl trapped under the beam. According to Ian and Ed, there was no way to free her. They had tried. We stood around assessing the piece of metal, trying to work out if there was anyway of shifting it. Time was not on the girl's side. She had no external injuries that we could see, but she was slowly being crushed to death. The beam was lying across her torso diagonally, pressing down on her so hard that her breathing had all but stopped. Ian and Ed said they had tried levering it with other bits of metal, had combined their strengths and tried to heave it, they had even tried to rip the seat from under the girl in the hope of pulling her free. Everything, they said, had conspired against them. The space they were working in was too cramped, they had inadequate tools; they were shattered mentally and physically. By the time I got to them they were on the verge of giving up. I asked them to make one final effort but Ed said, 'Trust me, it's pointless. We should go get help.'

I said, 'Help's on its way. Meantime, let's put our heads together and try and shift this thing.'

Ian started shuffling his feet. Radiating tiredness like an aura, he said, 'There's nothing more we can do here. And to be honest, I think I've done enough. The paramedics should be here any minute now.' He bowed his head, as if in shame, said, 'sorry,' then left. Ed lingered a while longer then he too left. I watched them go through the adjoining door and kept watching as they staggered along the carriage, so tired they could barely move.

I turned to the girl. The colour had drained from her lips and she was now hyperventilating. Feeling desperately sorry for her, I couldn't think of anything else to do but hold her hand. It was cold, clammy. Some of the people lying nearby looked at me pityingly, as if I was the one about to die. I continued to hold the girl's lifeless hand and began to wonder what her name was. All of a sudden that was really important to me. I would have asked her but I knew she wouldn't have been able to answer. She had almost gone now. Her eyes were closed and she had peaceful look on her face, as if she had resigned herself. Feeling helpless, I thought of something my brother was always saying to me: 'Take everything to the Lord in prayer. With him all things are possible.'

From sheer desperation, I offered up a silent prayer, begging and pleading for the girl's life to be spared. I hadn't prayed since I was a child, since the days when I was a choirboy. I had no belief in it then and had even less now. And yet I closed my eyes and prayed, holding the girl's hand throughout. When I'd finished, I opened my eyes and was amazed to see that she had opened hers, too. Not only that, she seemed to be smiling and, incredibly, she squeezed my hand. A baby could have squeezed it tighter, but even so I felt it. I don't know what came over me – my brother said later I was being moved by the Holy Ghost – but I got up and started looking again at the metal beam, determined that I would use up every last drop of my energy trying to move it. I looked at it every which way, walked around it, put both my hands on it and shoved it, put my back against it and tried to heave it, sat on the floor and tried to use my legs to dislodge it even a little: it was all useless. Sweating and angry, I was now engaged in a tremendous struggle. I forgot about the girl and the others lying dead and injured. This was now between me and that piece of metal. If it was the immovable object, I was the unstoppable force. I simply refused to be beaten. I racked my brain trying to find a solution.

Closing my eyes again, I started talking to myself: 'Think, Simon. Think.' I paced to and fro, to and fro. Unable to make the break-through, I screamed in frustration and started jumping up and down like a spoilt child. When I felt the carriage rock

I froze, my mind racing. Deep down in the pit of my stomach I knew I'd stumbled across a solution. Just to be sure, I jumped up and down a few more times and yes, the carriage rocked from side to side. And that's when I remembered: while I was down on the tracks, I had noticed that the front part of the carriage was slightly off the rail. If I could make it tilt a little further on to its side, then the upper part of the metal beam, the part wedged in the window, should come loose enough to allow me to pull it away and drag the girl to safety.

Excited, I moved down the carriage and jumped through the double doors back on to the track. Charles was still there. He was sitting beside Stuart, cradling his head. He saw me but said nothing but I didn't like the look of him, he was too hunched. I wondered for a moment if Stuart had died in his arms but I had no time to dwell on it. I stood back a bit to assess the state of the carriage. Just as I had remembered, it was slightly tilted on one side, away from where I stood. I could see the metal beam sticking out of the window above. The floor of the carriage was level with my head. To shift it, I would have to use my arms and shove it forward. Under normal circumstances, that would have been impossible, but with the carriage being off the rail slightly, I felt I had a small chance. Digging my heels into the gravel to secure my footing, I leaned forward and placed my hands against the side of the carriage so that my body was stretched out almost in a straight line. Summoning all my remaining strength, I pushed so hard I felt something give in my lower back. The pain was excruciating but the carriage had moved a bit so I gave it another shove, and then another, screaming at the top of my voice each time.

By now the sweat was pouring off me and I could barely see I was so dizzy. Every muscle in my body was shot. I had nothing left. When I looked up at the window and saw that the beam hadn't moved I slumped to the ground and started sobbing. I had neither the energy nor the will to go back into the carriage. The girl was probably long dead and I just couldn't face seeing her. Sitting there on the tracks, my face wet with tears, I saw something in my peripheral vision and turned to see a group of people running along the tracks towards me. They looked so hazy in the distance they could have been a mirage. I passed out before they got to me. Later, when I woke up in hospital, I found out they were paramedics.

Part One

When we arrived at the town hall Rhona and Sky started fussing over me like a couple of mother hens, their anxiety bringing out their natural rivalry. No sooner had Rhona straightened my tie than Sky was saying it looked better the way it was. Where Rhona was keen for me to make a good showing, present myself in the best light, Sky cautioned against putting on airs and advised me to be natural. This caused an argument between them and I was forced to act as referee, which increased my nerves even as I was trying to settle theirs. And all this was in full view of the Mayor, the invited guests and several national newspaper journalists

It was a small but decent turnout, about fifty people in total. The afternoon began with everyone milling around the high-ceilinged entrance hall, chatting in cliques and enjoying a pre-reception tipple of cheap white wine. Curiously, the middle-aged Mayor, who seemed weighed down as much by his chain of medallions as by his responsibilities, hardly had a word to say to me before things got under way proper. After an initial handshake and a brief summary of the afternoon's agenda, he abandoned me. And as if taking their lead from the big man, none of the other guests approached me either, not even the journalists. Maybe they thought it wasn't correct protocol, like speaking to the Queen without officially being invited to, but still it felt strange standing in a corner with Rhona and Sky and thinking I didn't belong there when in fact I was the guest of honour. Not since I first arrived in Duddenham had I experienced such a sharp sense of disconnection. At that moment I felt a pang of nostalgia for London like never before. It was physical, a kind of dull ache in the pit of my stomach, and what with the wine and my frayed nerves and the fact that I hadn't eaten a proper breakfast, I started to feel nauseous and feared that I might actually retch. Luckily the feeling died down, but it never went away completely and for the remainder of the afternoon I prayed that I wouldn't embarrass myself and everyone else by throwing up.

I spent the next two hours sitting at a long table on a podium in the company of the Mayor and a handful of other council officials. I felt uncomfortable sitting up there looking down on the guests. As I scanned their faces I wasn't sure that all of them were as taken with me as the Mayor had claimed. In fact most of them seemed quite indifferent to what was happening; even bored. And yet they had put on their best clothes and come along anyway. I know that had it not been in my honour, Rhona and Sky would never have attended such a dreary event. As it was, those two were sitting proudly in the front row, smiling up at me, as if I was about to receive the Nobel Prize.

Standing at a lectern, the Mayor kicked off the proceedings by thanking everyone for coming and mentioned, on my behalf, how much I appreciated it and how proud I was for such a strong show of support. I had told him beforehand that I would not be making a speech, so he was doing his best to speak for me without misrepresenting me. This required him to preface almost everything he said with, 'I'm sure Simon won't mind my saying,' or 'I'm sure Simon would agree with me when I say,' after which he would turn to me to get my assent and I would nod at him to carry on. After a few minutes I started to relax and allowed myself to be swept along on the tide of all his praise and plaudits. I believe I even exchanged a smile or two with Rhona and Sky.

All in all the Mayor did a very good job on me, except once when he said, 'I'm sure Simon would agree when I say that from the first day he arrived here he has been shown nothing but warmth and hospitality...' Not true, Mr Mayor. Not true at all.

When I first came to Duddenham, feeling lonely and practically wandering around with my chin on my chest, a time when I yearned, physically yearned, for a bit of human contact, I found the majority of the people I came across to be cold and standoffish. Yes they would smile and nod – when they were not openly gawking – but only in the most mechanical way and only in passing. They were certainly not interested in talking to me. For a bit of much-needed conversation I had to rely on the few words I was able to exchange each day with my local newsagent, a sprightly old guy called Len.

Even now, after seven years of being in the town, I had never been invited to a party or to a neighbour's house for dinner or even for a cup of tea. Then again, it worked both ways. What exactly had I done to try to meet people? Not very much. I once went to my local community centre – a prefab building on a piece of litter-strewn scrubland near my house – to see what community activities I might get involved in, but, snob that I am, I just couldn't bring myself to join the local bowling club or the bird watching society or to take part in the preparations for the annual sofa race, a spectacle that, had I not seen it with my own eyes, I wouldn't have believed. The truth was, the town had little to recommend it. It was the sort of place you drove through, or around, on your way to somewhere more enlivening. Of the few thousand inhabitants, all but a handful lived outside the town centre in crumbling, pebble-dashed houses or on drab, low-rise housing estates. It got few visitors, wasn't known for anything, had no famous sons or daughters. I discovered it purely by chance.

On my way to drop off a parcel – I was working as a deliveryman at the time – I took a wrong exit on the motorway and had to do a detour through the town centre. The shops along the high street told me I was in a deprived part of the country: Poundstretcher, Iceland, Mr Chippy's Chip Shop, Corals, Cash Converter. 'I could live here,' I thought, which says something about the state I was in at the time. A few days later I went back and checked into a B&B. The next day I began looking for work. It took me a week to find a job and a further week to find a house, which I still occupy. After his first visit to see me, Theodore shook his head and said, 'Why do this to yourself, bro? Why punish yourself like this?' But that wasn't how I saw it. Living in that town suited me just fine. It was cheap but more importantly, it allowed me to be whoever I wanted to be, to re-invent myself. In fact, I'd been feeling more peaceful and settled in my life than I had done in years.

After the bombing, my life, on every significant level, turned upside down. I became, as the saying goes, an overnight celebrity. I was held up as a hero, with my face plastered all over the local and national papers. Imagine that – me, a hero. It would have been frightening if it hadn't been so absurd. The upshot of this new-found fame was that suddenly everyone wanted a piece of me. I now had to contend with complete strangers approaching me in the street with requests to recount the gory details of my so-called heroics. To walk into my local pub was to be subjected to the kind of intrusive, in-your-face attention that would have sent Gandhi into a rage. A week after the bombing I was in there having a quick one with Dave when two old geezers who were sitting next to us leaned across and, without so much as a by-your-leave, practically demanded my autograph. When, with gritted teeth, I scribbled my illegible initials on their beer mats, one of them beamed at me and said, 'Who says there's no more heroes? God love you, son. God love you.' Of course Dave saw the whole thing as one big joke and spent the rest of the evening teasing me with an over the top rendition of the Superman theme tune, but I was struggling to see the funny side.

No-one likes to have their privacy invaded. It was nothing compared to the attitude of the press, though, especially the tabloids. No matter how many times I turned down their requests for an exclusive interview, which came with ever-increasing financial inducements, they refused to take no for an answer. At least they had finally decamped from my doorstep, but I knew that for as long as the bombing remained in the news – and it showed no signs of going away – they would keep calling me. They were nothing if not persistent. I

17

had changed my mobile number twice since the bombing but they always seemed to get hold of it.

After the Mayor had finished his address, we were shown a short video of recorded interviews given by some of the survivors of the bombing, including Stuart and Latonya, the girl who had been trapped under the beam. I had spoken to both of them since the bombing, they had contacted me to express their gratitude. In the video, Latonya described her escape as a miracle. According to her – and this was corroborated by the emergency services – my efforts to dislodge the beam had been successful. I had moved it, only very slightly, but enough for the paramedics to pull Latonya free. Several of her ribs had been crushed, and she'd suffered a lot of internal bleeding, but she was well on her to making a full recovery. Both she and Stuart claimed to owe me their lives. I felt utterly undeserving of such sentiments.

It came upon me without warning. Towards the end of the video my vision suddenly went hazy. Panicking, I blinked several times to try and regain focus, but if anything it made the problem worse. I didn't think anyone had noticed. The room had been darkened for the video, so I used that to my advantage and started rubbing my eyes. And then, as quickly as it had left me, my vision returned. But now there was another, more worrying problem. When I looked again at the screen I did not see what I had expected to see. Instead of the film we had been watching I saw something that made me get up and head for the exit. Outside the hall I was quickly joined by Rhona and Sky and not long after that by the Mayor and the other council officials. They found me leaning against a wall, shaking like a freezing puppy. I waved everyone away except Rhona and Sky. 'Let's get out of here,' I told them. Straightening up as best I could, I apologised to the Mayor and the others and we left. On the way home I suddenly remembered that the audience, including the assembled journalists, had been denied their Q&A session with me and that the Mayor was supposed to have presented me with the keys to the town.

We headed towards the town centre to get a cab, at my suggestion. The walk home was only about forty-five minutes, but I didn't feel up to it. It was a hot, sunny afternoon in August and I was sweaty and faint and desperate to get home. At one point Rhona insisted that I loosen my tie and unbutton my collar and every now and then Sky would ask if I wanted to stop and rest for a bit. To reach the cab rank we had to walk along the high street. As usual for a Saturday, it was clogged with shoppers and noisy, most of the noise coming from a three-piece brass band who always busked outside the Marie Curie charity shop. Normally I didn't mind them, but that afternoon their instruments sounded maddeningly loud and out of tune.

As we got to the rank I suddenly felt really thirsty. Sky offered to go into the nearby Greggs and get some drinks but I told her it was a waste of money. 'Blockbuster is only two doors down, remember? Dave's in today. Just tell him what you want and he'll put it on my account.' She went off and left me and Rhona to queue up. It was only then that Rhona asked me to explain what had had happened at the town hall. To avoid being overheard by the other people in the queue – some of them had recognised me and were trying not to stare – I whispered, 'Can we talk about it when we get home?' Rhona stroked my back and said, 'Sure.'

Just then Sky returned carrying three bottles of Fanta. She handed one to me, one to Rhona and kept one for herself. She was accompanied by Dave, who was wearing his Blockbuster uniform. Short and stocky, I'd always thought he looked like a bouncer. After kissing Rhona on the cheek, he looked me up and down and said, 'I hope you don't think you're getting out of your shift tomorrow.' I rolled my eyes. Rhona put her arms around Dave's shoulder and said, 'Any new games in?' He shook his head, ''Fraid not, love, nothing you'd be interested in anyway.'

A couple of cabs pulled up, people got into them, they pulled out again. We shuffled a little further along the pavement. Dave said to me, 'Never seen you suited and booted before. You look almost handsome.' That made Sky laugh. I was feeling too out of sorts to banter with Dave. I did my best but I couldn't muster the necessary bite. 'I see you've locked the store again during opening hours. That's against company policy isn't it?' Barely hiding his annoyance, Dave came back with, 'What are they gonna do, sack me? I wish they would.' We'd reached the head of the queue and our cab arrived, stopping directly in front of us. I stepped straight from the pavement into the front passenger seat, which had more room for my long legs. Through the open window, Dave said, 'Oh by the way, got a bone to pick with you, sir. How come I didn't get an invite to your big day?' It was an awkward moment. I felt it, Rhona and Sky felt it, even the cab driver felt it. I started stuttering but Dave said, 'Only joking you lemon. I'll see you tomorrow.' The cab driver visibly relaxed and said, 'We all set?'

Twenty minutes later the cab pulled up outside my house. Narrow, curved, tree-lined and deadly quiet, the contrast between my street and the town centre was marked. Just being in it made me feel better. I turned to Rhona and said, as a joke, 'Coming in? I tidied up specially.' She laughed. 'No, you're alright. I've made my yearly visit. That's plenty for me.' She had come round a few days earlier, for the first time in months, and only because she'd wanted to butter me up. As I got out of the cab she became serious. 'You gonna be OK?' I nodded and she added, 'Why not swing by later? I'll cook. You can bring booze.' I touched her arm through the open window and said, 'Done.' I then winked at Sky who smiled at me and said, 'Bring me a bottle of cider?' I looked at Rhona. 'It's up to you,' she said. The cab driver was getting impatient so I tapped twice on his roof and he drove off.

I got in, undressed and went and stood under the shower, amused at the thought of how much Rhona hated coming to my house. At first she had used the excuse of not wanting to leave Sky alone in the evenings, but it was no longer valid since Sky, at sixteen, was now capable of looking after herself and could stay at Trevor's if necessary. I'd once suggested that they come over more and occasionally spend the night but Rhona had claimed she didn't want to impose on me. Eventually I had it out with her and she admitted she found my house depressing. I had no defence. My house is depressing.

Two-storeys, brown, pebble-dashed, with rotting bay windows, a gravelled front yard used for the bins and a narrow back garden with a weed-choked lawn, it was by far the worst kept property in the street. And that was just the exterior. It was even worse on the inside. How many times had I told myself to change the stained shower curtain and the wonky toilet lid? How often had I sworn to throw out the broken down sofa and splash out on a new one? I could barely stand to look at the ancient net curtains, the moth-eaten drapes, the grey, threadbare carpet and the peeling, wood-chip wallpaper, and yet I did nothing about them. Even the landlord had said he was prepared to reimburse me for whatever I laid out, within reason, but not even that had stirred me into action. Initially I told myself that as a temporary stop I would be foolish to spend time and money on refurbishments, but when did temporary end and permanent begin? I'd lived in the house for seven years. Anyhow, since Rhona confessed that she couldn't stand the place, she rarely called round, despite the fact that we lived at opposite ends of the same street. I can't say I blamed her.

In structure, her house was identical to mine but in a much better state of repair and far more homely. She and Trevor had taken out several home improvement loans to do it up. As well as a new roof, they'd added an extension to the back that swallowed up a big piece of the garden but had put thousands on the market price. In summer, with the back door open, it was the coolest part of the house and functioned as both lounge and dining room. It had dark heavy drapes on the windows, wooden floors, a ceiling fan, a three-seater upholstered sofa-bed stuffed with coloured cushions, a home entertainment system that included a game console, and a pine-wood dining table with four matching chairs. Rhona loved it so much she seemed to spend all her spare time there, mostly playing computer games but occasionally reading – she liked Ann Cleeves – or watching TV. Sky didn't like it as much, said it looked like an old people's home, but I was with Rhona in thinking that it had a relaxing effect which no other room in the house possessed.

Whenever I stayed over and didn't fancy going to sleep early, I'd hang out there watching TV and snacking, making regular runs to the kitchen and the toilet. The next morning Sky would come down, usually on her way to school, and find me asleep on the sofa-bed. She'd never leave before putting a sheet or a blanket over me, depending on the time of year. If I was still asleep when Rhona came down, I'd jump up and start clearing away my half-eaten snacks and restoring the room to its former state. Rhona was house-proud, she liked her living space to be just so, whereas I was a slob. It was one reason why she and I had decided not to move in together. Another was the desire to maintain our independence. Two years after her bitter marriage split, she wanted to avoid becoming too entangled with another man, both materially and emotionally, and I was wary of literally stepping into the space vacated by her ex. We were comfortable with the arrangement, which wasn't so much casual as informal, but we knew we couldn't go on like that forever, we knew the situation would have to change eventually. And it had.

Since the bombing, there'd been a slight but noticeable shift and we had moved a bit closer together. The media attention had left me feeling exposed and vulnerable and Rhona had been very supportive, especially in the first couple of weeks after the bombing when I was having counselling for post-traumatic stress. I'd made her proud, which hadn't always been the case. My lack of worldly ambition used to be a source of contention between us. She thought I could do better and could never understand why I didn't demand more from life. I wasn't made to feel inadequate, but every now and then, as a way to motivate me, she would talk about how Trevor had started from nothing and now ran his own firm of builders. 'If he can do that, and he's a bird-brain, imagine what someone with your intelligence could achieve if you go at it.' These references to Trevor always put me on the defensive. She claimed to hate the man yet admired his achievements? It made no sense to me until I realised that everything she did was in some way designed to impress Trevor, to make him see that she could live without him. If I was a success, she could hold her head up in his presence, and that explained why her attitude towards me had changed since the bombing. Trevor had a bit of money but I had achieved something much better than that. I had acquired fame. That it had happened accidentally and as a result of a terribly tragedy seemed of no consequence to Rhona.

Trevor. I hated to think of myself as being in competition with him. I thought he was pathetic, immature. He and Rhona were divorced yet he wouldn't leave her alone. Once I came on the scene, he seemed to go out of his way to make things difficult for us, regularly showing up at the house unannounced and demanding to speak with Sky. Rhona had no right or wish to deny him his legal visitation rights, but anything outside of that she flatly refused. It was an ongoing battle and Sky was caught in the middle. She loved both her parents but was old enough and sensible enough to know that they didn't work together as a couple. In an ideal world, she wanted to divide her time between them equally, but it wasn't practical.

During the divorce she had been asked to choose which of them she wanted to live with. Not unnaturally, she chose her mother, though she felt guilty about it. Trevor didn't take the snub lightly. He accused Rhona of poisoning his daughter's mind against him and they'd been at each other ever since. I tried as best I could to stay out of it, and I tried to be civil to Trevor. I even invited him out for a drink once. I had gone round to his house to make the offer but he wouldn't let me in. Standing on the doorstep, he waited till I'd finished speaking, then said, 'What sort of bloke are you? Why don't you fuck off and get your own family?' I was about to reply but he slammed the door in my face. Since then, we'd barely exchanged two words. I told Rhona about the incident and she called him a child, said he was spiteful and vindictive and that I should try to avoid him. That wasn't easy. I was part of his life, whether I liked it or not. Unless I stopped seeing Rhona, which wasn't going to happen, I had to deal with him.

Mostly I was able to rise above his pettiness, but occasionally I allowed myself to be dragged down to his level. Like the other day. He'd come round to get Sky for the weekend and I answered the door to him. He was his usual charming self. 'Fuck you doing 'ere? Told you, don't want you in my house. Now come on, sling it!' I stepped back a bit, in case he tried to put his hands on me, but Rhona appeared in the nick of time and averted a potentially worse confrontation. 'Give it a rest, Trevor,' she said, wearily. 'This isn't your house any more, remember? Sky! Get a move on.' Sky showed up and, familiar with the scene, rolled her eyes at the three of us. 'Honestly,' she said, then flounced out. Before he turned and followed her, Trevor fired me a parting shot: 'Won't tell you again. Don't want you in my house. Got it?' Rhona was about to say something but I shut the door before she had a chance.

Feeling much better after showering and changing my clothes, I went round to see Rhona. It was about six o'clock in the evening and the temperature, though still hot enough for an outbreak of flying ants, had fallen to a manageable level. Rhona cooked a pasta bake with a green leaf side salad, one of her favourite dishes, and we ate it in the extension, the ceiling fan whirring above our heads. To accompany the meal, I had beer, Rhona had white wine and Sky had a pear cider, a reward for all the studying she'd been doing ahead of her next round of exams. In the middle of dinner, Rhona asked whether I had thought any more about selling my story. We'd had an argument about it a few days before so I was surprised she brought up. 'Not really, no.' It was a lie. I had all but made up my mind, but I resented the way she was badgering me over it. She seemed disappointed with my answer and started sulking while trying to give the impression that she wasn't.

Immediately after dinner, Sky went to her room to speak to her friend on the phone. She, the friend, came round about an hour later. Her name was Chloe, and, like Sky, she was thin and fashion conscious. That evening she was wearing gold hot-pants and black, patent leather Doc Martens boots. She came in and said hello to us then went up to Sky's room and didn't come out again till she was ready to go home, around nine thirty. Sky was never seen again that night, at least not by me. At eleven o'clock Rhona went up to say goodnight and apparently found her fast asleep, her Blackberry in her hand. Later, with the door to the extension locked against Sky,

Rhona and I had muted sex on the sofa bed. I wasn't really in the mood, it was the second week of the football season and I had hoped to watch Match of the Day, but Rhona, who always got randy after drinking wine, never stopped pawing and pulling at me till I gave in.

Afterwards, she asked me again to explain what had happened at the town hall, saying that she had been shaken up to see me looking so frightened. 'It was all a bit much, really. Hearing those people talk, seeing all those images again. I felt like my nose was being rubbed in it. Too many bad memories, I suppose.' She accepted my explanation, saying it was a logical reaction, but what I'd told her was only partly true. Yes, the occasion had got to me, had brought me back to the horror of the bombing, but I didn't mention the other things I'd seen, the sudden, jarring visions that had flashed into my mind. I used to get them all the time but hadn't had one in years. Why they should have returned now, and with such intensity, was a mystery too deep for me to fathom, but it felt as if the two things, the memory of the bombing and the visions from the past, were somehow linked, if not in reality then at least in my mind.

Whatever had caused their return I hadn't been able to shake them all day. Like the after tremors of a massive earthquake, the later ones had less of a devastating effect on me but were no less vivid. I'd actually had one at the dinner table but somehow managed to conceal my reactions from Rhona and Sky. They were having a conversation about Sky's grandmother on her father's side. Sky had promised to visit her but had forgotten and wanted to get her a gift to make things up but couldn't decide on what. Rhona said, 'Flowers.

You can never go wrong with those.' Sky made a face and said, 'Boring.' And that's when the visions began. Clear, detailed, horrifying. I saw Mitch. He was staring at me; he wanted to harm me. Benjy was there, too. He had another kind of look in his eyes, the scared look of someone who was in over his head and didn't know how to get out. They were both naked. I saw the room. It was bare, dark, the curtains were drawn. There was a smell in the air, something fetid, rotten, evil. Mitch was arguing with me, swearing at me, threatening me. My head was spinning. Too much coke. I was having to keep my eye on Mitch, in case he tried to jump me, but I was losing it, losing my nerve, losing control of the situation, losing my will to live. I wanted to put the gun to my head and pull the trigger but I couldn't do it. And that's where the vision ended. More things happened that night, a lot more, but I wasn't getting any of it. I'd been blocking so effectively, for so long, the full picture was taking time to re-emerge. I didn't want to think about any of it and I certainly didn't want to tell Rhona about it. I couldn't tell her or anybody.

* * *

The following morning, on my way to work, I popped into Len's, bought a few of the tabloids and stood in a corner reading them. The story of the aborted reception featured prominently in all of them. The headlines were a variation on *'Bomb Hero Honoured'* and each article mentioned the fact that I'd taken ill and that the reception had been cut short. No surprises there. What did surprise me was the extent to which the journalists had embellished their stories.

One paper stated that I had collapsed on stage. Another said I had cried out in anguish before running from the room like, and I quote, 'the Elephant Man fleeing his tormentors.' Still another had it that I went ashen before keeling over backwards on my chair. As I read, I kept shaking my head. Even the quotes were unsubstantiated. I couldn't believe the number of townsfolk who, lying through their teeth just to get their names in the papers, had been quoted as having had personal dealings with me over the years. And then there were the pictures, which made me look as if I was about to stab someone. I couldn't have appeared more threatening if I had been auditioning for the role of 'Thug Number One' in the latest idiotic gangster flick. Normally the sight of a black man in a daily newspaper looking menacing would have caused me to be no more than mildly irritated, but to see myself so portrayed almost made me call the Press Complaints Commission. When I considered everything as a whole – the inaccurate reporting, the insidiously racist photographs, the unchecked quotes – it was little wonder I was so wary of getting involved with the media.

I made sure to arrive for my shift ten minutes early. Dave was impatient to leave but when he saw that I'd brought the papers, he stayed behind for a while and read a couple of the articles, whistling the Superman theme tune throughout. Eventually he finished reading and said, 'Right, I'm off. Don't work too hard now.' We looked out across the empty store. Sundays were normally quiet, which is why I always volunteered to work them. As soon as Dave left, I put on *Shawshank Redemption* then went and made myself a cup of tea. My shift started at midday and finished at eight. In that time I served a total of six customers and watched three films, my feet up on the counter.

When I first started working at Blockbuster, I did so hoping that I would get to sit around all day watching films. It's the assumption everyone has about the video store employee and it was the one I had when I applied for the job. I was pleased to discover there was some truth to the myth. I got to watch a lot of films, but after three years I was beyond saturation point and had actually gone off them, especially the big, overblown, Hollywood rubbish that we specialised in. And since I no longer enjoyed that benefit, it had become clear to me that there was very little else to recommend the job. In fact I found it so silly that sometimes it was all I could do not to stop in the middle of my shift and laugh out loud. Take my job title for example. I was officially a Customer Services Representative, or CSR for short. Quite apart from being vague, it was misleading. The 'S' in the title should really have stood for 'Sales', since a significant part of what I did was trying to flog things to people. The customers could barely get in the door before I was bombarding them with special offers of one sort or another. 'Did you know that if you rent another movie, you can get a third free? Also, our popcorn is on offer at the moment. Two for two pounds. Wha' d'you say?' Not surprisingly, I had a few people telling me where to stick my offers.

These humiliations were starting to take their toll. I knew it was only a matter of time before I quit the job, I knew I couldn't go on doing it forever, but until then I tried to concentrate on the perks. There were several. First, the hours were flexible. If I didn't fancy working, I could take a few days off, provided I could arrange cover. Second, the job was physically undemanding. I'd had enough of back-breaking work and was pleased to discover that the only lifting I was expected to do was when the boxes of confectionery arrived each week and had to be stored away. I could handle that. I treated it as a bit of exercise, which was needed given that I spent most of my shift sitting behind the counter drinking cups of tea and eating biscuits. Third, I didn't have a boss telling me what to do. Dave, at thirty-five, was my junior by a couple of years, but he was also my manager. In practise this meant nothing since he never gave me orders. Whenever we worked together, all he ever wanted to do was talk about football. Away from work we had become close – we went to the pub a couple of times a week – and I regarded him as my only friend in Duddenham.

She'd hate to hear me calling it a perk, but I met Rhona at Blockbuster. She used to come in to the store at least three times a week. I remember she struck me as being different from the other female customers in that she didn't go in for idiotic rom-coms, but was in fact into computer games. And I don't mean the namby-pamby type of game that so many of the other women were into, but the ultra-violent, shoot-em-and-chop-em-to-death variety that was almost exclusively the preserve of the guys. Over time our banter became increasingly flirtatious. I found her confidence sexy, or was it the fact that she regularly wore super tight jeans that flattered her long legs and pert buttocks? She and I still joked about the time we first spoke to each other. While I was busy trying to interest her in one of our many laughable offers – two packets of cheese puffs and a movie for a fiver, I believe it was – she had her eyes on my pecs.

31

She no longer came into the store. There was no need. She called and told me which games she wanted and I brought them over after work. Free of charge. I teased her about the fact that I had saved her thousands of pounds over the years, but I was careful not to go too far as she was very sensitive on the subject of money. Before we got together, a significant percentage of her earnings had been spent on her gaming obsession. How she managed that and kept the wolves from her door, I had no idea. Even now, with all the savings she made through me, I wondered how she coped financially. The little she earned as a dental receptionist could barely keep her and Sky in food, let alone pay all her bills. I knew that Trevor made a contribution to the mortgage and to Sky's upkeep, but apart from that, she had to do everything on her meagre wages. Money was a constant worry for her. More than anything she wanted to be financially independent of Trevor. 'I'd love to buy him out of this house,' she once told me, 'and if I had my way, I wouldn't accept a penny of his money for Sky.' To this end, unknown to me, she had been working on a plan.

A few days before I was honoured at the town hall, she had called me from the surgery, as she often did during her lunch break, to say she had something she wanted to discuss with me. She didn't want to give any details over the phone, but I was curious and I pressed her to give me something, anything, a clue. She refused, was being deliberately cryptic. For a crazy moment I half-suspected that she was plotting to rob a bank and wanted me as her accomplice. I almost said as much. Sensing my frustration, she said, 'Don't worry, I'll tell you everything tonight. But at yours. Don't want that bloomin' nosey daughter of mine eavesdropping on us. I'll come over around six if it's all right with you.' As soon as she mentioned coming over I knew she was going to ask for something, a favour, something requiring me to put myself out on her behalf. If she had to stoop so low as to come to my house, it had to be something significant.

On the day she was due to come round I made sure to get up early so I could do a bit of cleaning. It had been weeks since I last tidied up and I was daunted by the size of the task facing me. It certainly felt strange to be breaking a sweat trying to get the place ready, as though I were expecting the visit of some foreign dignitary. There was so much to do I had to begin the clean-up in the morning before I went to work and rush back home immediately afterwards to complete it. And even then I was still doing last minute bits and pieces when Rhona showed up.

She arrived a few minutes early, which increased my already jangly nerves. At the front door she handed me not one, but two bottles of red wine. When we entered the living room, her eyes widened. 'Good God! Someone's been busy. Wait,' she had a quick look around, 'I'm in the right house, aren't I?' It's strange how the things we first admire about a person end up becoming the very things we loathe. I used to find her sarcasm entertaining, now I found it dull. 'Funny.' I said, and went off to the kitchen to open one of the bottles of wine.

When I returned Rhona was sitting, or should I say reclining, on the sofa. She had one leg up under her bum and was flicking through my cable listings magazine. As I entered the room she said, 'All this stuff on TV and not one decent programme anywhere. And you wonder why I'm into computer games.' She tossed the magazine aside. I handed her a glass of wine and sat down beside her at what I thought was a safe enough distance. She noticed the gesture, but let it go without comment. 'Cheers,' she said, looking deep into my eyes. She had quite a penetrating stare, unnerving, but I didn't avert my eyes as I was determined not to be wrong footed by her. She was being at her most seductive, evidenced by the low cut top that exposed her ample cleavage and by the fact that she had practically showered in perfume. The room was filled with her floral scent. 'Cheers,' I replied. We touched glasses, put them to our lips, and then I came to the point. 'So come on. Out with it.' She smiled. 'OK. But you have to promise that you'll hear me out before you say anything.' That confirmed it. I was not going to like what she had to say. 'Do you promise?' she said, in her best little girl voice. She even gave a little pout for good measure. I sighed. 'Yes, yes, I promise. Now get on with it.'

She said she had been mulling over my situation with the press and their constant requests for interviews. While she understood my reluctance to have anything to do with them, while she was proud of the fact that I wanted to protect my privacy and, by extension, the people in my life who might also be affected, the fact remained that I was in a position to capitalise on my fame and I should seriously consider selling my story to the papers. It was a once in a lifetime opportunity and if I didn't exploit it I would live to regret it. I thought she had finished but she quickly added, 'And if you don't want to do it for yourself, then do it for me. You know what it would mean for me to be free of Trevor. You'd be helping me. Sky, too.' So that was it. She wasn't interested in my welfare, but her's and her daughter's. I lost my temper, we rowed and she stormed out, calling me a fool and other names besides. Not long after she left I began to feel guilty for the way I had reacted. Once I had calmed down and looked at the thing rationally, I could see the sense in what she was suggesting. The sums of money being offered for my story would have made a significant difference to my life. It would have enabled me to do those things I'd been dreaming about for years: buy my own home, set up a business of some kind, go travelling. All that was now in reach.

In fairness I had been thinking about selling my story long before Rhona made her suggestion but had been delaying it in the hope that the interest in the bombing would die away and the decision would be taken out of my hands. In fact the story, which was now being universally referred to as 7/7, had gathered such momentum that I was now getting phone calls from all sorts of people wanting to exploit my celebrity: join this movement, become the public face of that charity, support this cause. In this area alone I could have written my own cheques. These people were prepared to pay handsomely for the privilege of using my face and name. But I feared getting involved with them almost as much as I feared the media. For one thing, a lot of the stuff would have involved appearing on TV, which I would simply not consider under any circumstances, and for another, it would have meant going to London. I hadn't been back since the bombing and was very nervous about doing so. But I hadn't ruled out the possibility of giving one big interview to either a newspaper or magazine. It wouldn't have required too much of me to answer some questions and pose for a few photographs and I felt sure I could dictate when and where.

When I thought about it like that it almost began to seem easy and I felt foolish for not having done it already. Rhona had been right. In her cack-handed, self-serving way, she had helped me make up my mind.

Two days after the reception at the town hall I had gone back there, at the request of the Mayor, to complete the key-giving ceremony. That time there was only a handful of people present, the ceremony took place in a nondescript ante-room, and the only media in attendance was a reporter from the local weekly paper who waited patiently for everything to finish and then, with cheeky glint in his eye, asked if I would consider giving him an exclusive interview. When I turned him down, with a smile and a pat on his young, dandruffed shoulders, he said, 'Oh come on, Simon, where's your sense of local pride?'

After leaving the town hall I went round to see Rhona and Sky. They hadn't been able to attend the rescheduled ceremony due to work and boyfriend commitments respectively and were keen to hear news of how it had gone. When I said, 'Nothing to write home about,' they were visibly relieved not to have missed out on anything. When I showed them my 'key', an outsized thing made from aluminium, they laughed. Sky then told me that she had bought one of the papers that morning to show the article to Chloe. Apparently Chloe thought I looked 'well fit' and that given the chance she would 'do' me.

At the reception I'd been approached by a man called Richard Bottomley who claimed to be an agent. He had, he said, travelled from London to meet me in person and he wanted to make me a promise. 'If you allow me to represent you,

I'll make you a fortune.' He was in his early thirties, with a fleshy, slightly pockmarked face. He was wearing a sharp pin-stripe suit and shiny brogues and seemed very sure of himself without being cocky. I was impressed by him and made a point of telling him so, even as I was turning down his offer. Fortunately I had kept his card. Now feeling guilty at the way things had gone with Rhona, I decided to call him. When he heard my voice, he shrieked with excitement down the phone and a day later he came to visit me again.

We went to my local pub for lunch and he talked excitedly about what he described as my 'earning potential'. I must admit that he seduced me with all the figures he bandied about which, in my current financial situation, wasn't saying very much. It didn't take long for us to reach an agreement. Before we parted company he made me sign a contract, which he had been presumptuous enough to bring with him, and then told me to leave everything in his 'capable hands'.

'From now on, you don't have to do anything. If any offers come your way, let me know and I'll deal with them. Direct all enquiries to me, all right? Now, then, as far as the interview's concerned, I'll contact the editors myself to see who's offering the most dosh. My bet is that it'll be one of the Sunday tabloids. You wouldn't mind that would you?'

I did mind. I minded very much, but at that stage I just wanted to grab the money and run.

'No problem,' I replied. 'But I've got a couple of stipulations. They have to come to me and I get final say on any photos they use.' Richard made a quick note of my demands then said, 'The press are usually very sensitive on the issue of editorial control, for obvious reasons, but I'll see what I can do.'

Richard came up trumps. For an exclusive interview, the Sunday Mirror offered me a hundred grand. I could hardly believe it. Even without Richard's ten per cent commission that still left me a tidy sum. The paper had initially offered eighty thousand but, using the other papers' interest as a bargaining tool, Richard had persuaded them to raise their offer. 'They really want your story. I can't be sure of the exact angle, but from what they said, I think they're keen to hear about those moments between you and the girl.'

'Why those moments in particular?'

'As I said, I can't be sure, but my guess is that they want to focus on what made you stay with her so long and how you found the strength to move the carriage.' He laughed down the phone then went on, 'You're a hero now, but by the time they're finished, you'll be a super-hero. We might have to get you a pair of tights and a cape.'

'Oh please. Don't you start.'

Now that I'd made the decision, I felt even more nervous and conflicted. Instead of withdrawing from the spotlight, I was now consciously stepping into it. And for money. I was proud that I would now be able to help Rhona in her ongoing struggle to get out from under her bullying ex-husband, but if I was being totally honest, that was a by-product of my decision to sell my story. In a strange way, I felt deserving of all the attention I'd been getting. For once in my miserable life I had done something to be proud of, and I wouldn't have been human if I didn't wanted some kind of recognition for my actions, some kind of praise.

The *Mirror* interview took place a week later at my flat. Once again I attempted a bit of tidying up before the journalist arrived. In the end the effort was wasted as the interview was conducted in my back garden. Having spent the previous night in a stuffy B&B near the town centre, the journalist – a straggly-haired forty-something woman called Susie Lowencrantz – was keen to sample a bit of the early-morning sunshine. She arrived at nine a.m. sharp and we talked almost non-stop till midday. She began by asking me about my life before I moved to Duddenham and I spun her yarn about a guy who had been born and brought up in a tough neighbourhood of London, who'd left school early and who, after years of doing 'nothing in particular', had grown tired of life in London and decided to sample the waters elsewhere. 'But why this place?' asked Lowencrantz, to which I replied, 'I was looking for a change, somewhere out of London, somewhere cheap.'

Backtracking slightly, she asked me to provide more details of my childhood, at which point I became extremely wary of her. Why was she so keen to know about my past? Was she up to something? Was there was more to her than met the eye?

'There's not much else to tell. Like I said, I went to a normal secondary school, left at sixteen, looked for work, couldn't find any and started signing on. Between that time and when I came here, I've been in and out of work. I'm working at the moment.'

She didn't seem convinced but I'd to put an edge to my voice, making it clear that I wasn't delving any further into my past. She scribbled my response and asked, 'Where do you work?'

'Blockbuster.'

Her eyes widened in surprise, which was how people usually reacted when I mentioned my job.

'You enjoy the work?' she asked, trying to keep the judgement out of her voice. The more she spoke, the more I disliked her.

'Not really. I used to, but now I hate it. I'll probably get fired after saying this, but even a chimp could do that work.'

'Why don't you leave if you hate it so much?'

'I'm going to.'

From then on her demeanour seemed to shift, she became more focussed, her questions became more specific and they were all to do with the bombing. She wanted blood and guts, she wanted gore, she wanted graphic details to titillate her readers. And so, playing the game, I gave her enough to keep her happy but held back from the truly horrific stuff. As Richard had thought, she asked me to describe the time I had spent with Stuart and Latonya and made me talk her through my efforts to move the carriage. She didn't seem to care how difficult it was for me to dredge it all up again. She was no shrink. She was a hard-nosed hack who'd come to do a job and was not going to allow sentiment to get in the way.

When I started talking about Stuart and how I'd had to bind his legs, I began to shake visibly at the memory, but Lowencrantz either didn't notice or she did and ignored it. She also asked me about Mohammad Sidique Khan.

'You say you saw him?'

I nodded, no longer willing to co-operate with what had now turned into an interrogation. She asked me to describe him, which I did, to the best of my memory, and afterwards she said, 'And how do you feel about what he did, what they did?'

40

I didn't know what to say besides, 'It was wrong.'

She noted my answer, taking a little too long over it. I couldn't wait for her wrap things up and I realised I'd made a huge mistake inviting her into my house. At last she said, 'OK, I think I've got enough. Just to remind you that the photographer'll be here day after tomorrow. He'll contact you directly.' She folded her notepad and switched off her Dictaphone. I observed her for a few moments as she hastily stuffed everything into her bag. She had what she wanted and suddenly seemed in a great hurry to get away. Just as she got up to leave I said, 'You didn't ask what I'm gonna do with the money you're paying me. The reader might like to know that, don't you reckon?' It was a sly dig but I couldn't help myself, I wanted to see her squirm a bit. She flashed me a condescending smile and said, 'I'm afraid not.'

'Why? That not part of the story, too?'

'Yes, but it's not a part the reader's interested in.'

* * *

I used my next shift with Dave to hand in my notice. It was a Friday evening, one of our busiest times. The customers were coming in by the minute, renting their films for the weekend and taking advantage of our special offers. Ideally I'd have waited till a more quiet time to make the announcement but I was keen to get the thing over and done with in case I changed my mind. I'd been in that position before, on the verge of leaving, only to back track out of fear. Jobs as cushy as those didn't grow on trees, which made it both a blessing and a curse: the ease of the work is what had trapped me.

Later that evening, while we were tidying up ahead of closing, Dave said he was happy that I was leaving. 'At least one of us is escaping, eh?' He had been at Blockbuster for eight years, and whilst he had often thought about quitting, he had so far lacked the courage to go through with it.

Trying to console him I said, 'Well at least you made manager.'

'Big deal. I get almost the same money as before but with three times the responsibility. I never thought I'd say this, but sometimes I miss being a CSR. You guys don't know you're alive.'

For a moment he went almost misty-eyed with nostalgia. And then he snapped out of it.

'But you're out. You're free. We should celebrate.'

I'd been feeling guilty since he mentioned not being invited to the reception and it felt like a good moment to apologise. 'Sorry about the other day.' He looked puzzled, so I explained.

After he'd heard me out, he said, 'Don't worry. I was working that day, anyway. Remember?'

'I know, but you could have booked it off if I'd given you notice. I don't know what I was thinking.'

He slapped me on the back and said, 'You're not gonna get all mushy on me are you? I hate mush.'

I smiled and he went round the back to put the alarm on. While he was gone I started thinking about our friendship. It was a strange one. We were close without being intimate. We didn't confide in each other or speak about anything of real importance. Though we lived, roughly, in the same area, I'd never been to his house and he'd never been to mine. We went to the pub, usually after work, sank a few pints while either watching football or talking about it, then went home. I didn't need anything more from him, and until he made that comment about the reception, I had assumed he felt the same way. He hadn't given me the slightest indication that he was interested in going, even though I had talked to him about it. To me he was the ideal friend, respectful of your space without being standoffish. He had never pried into my personal life or history and I had taken that to mean that he would like me to extend him the same courtesy.

In the beginning, we had provided each other with the basic facts our lives and things had never really moved on from there. I was from London, I had an older brother who was a Christian, my parents had retired and moved back to Jamaica, I had come to Duddenham for a change of scenery and a lower cost of living. He was born and raised in Duddenham and had spent most of his life there, he lived alone, he was close to his parents and saw them daily, he had always worked and always in retail, he had two friends he had known since school. I'd met them but had never socialised with them as Dave liked to keep us apart. One was an old flame called Stacie, a sullen, peroxide blonde whose roots were always showing, and the other was a guy called Paul, a biker who wore leathers all year round. They sometimes came into the store to get free rentals on Dave's account. If Dave was on shift, they'd stay and talk with him a while; if not, they couldn't get out of the store fast enough, especially if I was working. I had the impression that they didn't like me, that they saw me as some kind of rival for Dave's attention. He was that type, he had the ability to make you feel like the most important person in his life. That's certainly how he had made me feel, before the bombing but even more so after it. He was proud of what I'd done, but, in keeping with the nature of our friendship, the only way he could show it without causing us embarrassment or inflating my ego, was to poke fun at me. Rhona thought he was just being jealous, but I knew better, I knew that the more cutting his put-down, the deeper his affection.

A couple of evenings after I told him I was quitting my job, we went to one of our regular haunts for a few pints. It had been a while since we'd gone for a drink together and I'd forgotten just how much I enjoyed it. For midweek, the place was quite busy. As we walked in, a couple of the regulars nodded and smiled at me but not everyone in the pub was happy to see me. Trevor was in that night, sitting in a corner with a friend. When he saw me he all but hissed. I said to Dave, 'There's a bad smell in here tonight. Let's go somewhere else.' He spotted Trevor and said, 'Why the hell should we? Last time I checked, this weren't his pub.' And with that he practically marched me up to the bar and ordered the first round from Sabina, the young Polish bar girl.

Dave and I made sure to sit as far away from Trevor as possible, but such was the layout of the pub that we couldn't completely avoid seeing him or vice versa. Trevor and I spent a lot of time giving each other dirty looks. Dave did his best to occupy my attention, but no matter what topic of conversation he tried to interest me in – Champions League football, the latest gossip about the other staff at Blockbuster, the parlous state of the rental film industry in the age of illegal downloads – I just kept eyeballing Trevor. In the end Dave got frustrated. 'Just ignore him, will ya? The bloke's a waste of space.' I downed the last of my Guinness and said, 'You're right. Same again?' Dave nodded and I went off to the bar. While Sabina pulled the pints, I couldn't help myself and shot a quick glance in Trevor's direction. He noticed, gave me the finger, then he and his mate started chuckling like a couple of five-year-olds. I don't know why it should have happened then, and not on some previous occasion, but something in me snapped and I strode over to where Trevor was sitting and said, 'You got something to wanna say to me?' His friend said, 'Look, let's all calm down, eh?' Trevor then stood up. We were practically standing nose-to-nose. I could smell the booze on his breath. In weight and height, we were about the perfect match. For a few moments neither of us spoke, and then he said, 'Why don't you fuck off back to where you came from?'

'You what?'

'You heard. You're not welcome round here.'

'And yet I've just been given the key to the town. It's hanging above the bed in your ex-wife's bedroom.'

His nostrils flared. 'I'm warning you, don't push me.'

'Or else what?' He clenched his fists and stared at me. He was all ready to go but then seemed to have a change of heart.

'Your problem is you're blind. You can't see what's right in front of your nose. You can't see that Rhona's only using you to get back at me. I could have her back like that…' he snapped his fingers, '…but she can go and do one. If it wasn't for Sky I wouldn't go anywhere near that filthy slag.'

I punched him flush on the jaw. He staggered backwards like a man who'd had one too many and fell flat on his back.

Sabina screamed from behind the counter, which alerted everyone else in the pub to what was happening. Dave came rushing to my side. I knew that if it kicked off he'd probably come up short, but having him next to me was reassuring all the same. I stood waiting for Trevor's friend to do something but, obviously afraid, he backed away and started trying to revive his still prone friend. Trevor swore, brushed him aside and staggered to his feet, holding his jaw. He then tried to come at me but this time his friend held on to him and simply refused to let go, as if he feared for Trevor's life. Dave and I stood and waited to see what would happen next.

By now a handful of other drinkers had gathered around and one woman said to me, 'Go on now, leave it. It's over.' Like an adult who steps in to separate two warring kids, her words brought matters to a close. I said to Dave, 'Told you there was a bad smell in here. Can we go now?' He didn't need another invitation. We turned and walked away. Just as we were about to leave Trevor shouted, 'This isn't over you black cunt!' I immediately turned around, ready to do some serious damage now, and it took the combined force of Dave and the other customers to prevent me from having my way. Trevor was standing a few tantalising feet away, leering at me, satisfied with himself for having evened the score, if only verbally. I wanted to smash his teeth down his throat, but in the end I wriggled free of my captors and stepped outside. I gulped down a few quick draughts of the humid night air and then, accompanied by a very concerned-looking Dave, set off home.

I walked Dave to his flat, which took me completely out of my way. When I finally got in it was after midnight and

I went straight to bed. I needn't have bothered. Sleep just wouldn't come. I couldn't stop thinking about Trevor and what I wanted to do to him but after a while my anger burned out and I began to reflect on why I had gone to the pub in the first place. I had done it. I was leaving Blockbuster. I had taken the big step. The money I was set to receive from the paper had been the deciding factor but I hadn't mentioned that to Dave out of respect for his situation. He didn't need to hear that I was getting almost five times his annual salary in one go and could afford the luxury of taking a few months off work before deciding my next move. In the pub earlier he'd asked me how I intended to cope for money while looking for a new job and, jokingly, I'd said, 'I'm gonna sponge off you, of course.'

Still unable to sleep, I got out of bed and went into the living room and put the TV on. Flicking through the channels I settled on a cop thriller. It held my interest for about twenty minutes and then I got bored and switched it off. I fell asleep, still on the sofa, around two a.m. I had my usual nightmare. I saw Stuart lying on the tracks. After sawing both his legs off he handed me the saw and invited me to do the same with mine, laughing at me and calling me a coward when I start to run away. Next I saw myself in the bombed out carriage, surrounded by cadavers, maggots squirming from their eyes. One of them, who sometimes looked like Latonya and at other times like Theodore, was pointing a crossbow at me, getting ready to fire. I had to keep dodging and ducking, waiting for the moment when I was hit, but it never came. I woke up, as I always did at that point, gasping for breath, my heart hammering in my chest. I sat up, looked around. The front room was in darkness.

Convinced I could see shapes lurking in the corners, I got up and switched on the light and felt silly when I saw that there was nothing in the room but the usual items: the broken down sofa and the matching armchair, the knick-knacks on the mantelpiece, the torn paper shade covering the lightbulb, the TV in its plywood cabinet. I decided to go back to bed, thinking that a change of rooms might bring about a change in my mood. The opposite happened.

While lying in bed, with the radio on as a distraction, the visions started. Just as they had at the reception, and later at Rhona's, they suddenly flashed into my mind. The oppressively dark room. The horrible smell. Mitch and Benjy with no clothes on. Mitch desperate to attack me but wary of the gun in my hand. Benjy looking scared and unsure what to do. These visions, coming so soon after the nightmare, gave me violent convulsions. Thinking I was about to die, I had to get up and walk around to try to rid myself of the terrors. I paced about the house for more than an hour, going from room to room, my senses heightened, my nerves shredded, paranoid and jittery. I'd never felt more alone in my life. I almost called Rhona, but didn't want to disturb her ahead of her shift at the surgery, which was only a few hours away. I would have called Theodore but I had burdened him so much over the years with my problems I just didn't have the heart to weigh him down further. The poor guy deserved a break. That only left Dave. I knew he would have been happy and flattered that I had turned to him in a crisis yet I didn't because my ego wouldn't allow it. He had just seen me lay out Trevor. I couldn't then call him to say I was feeling scared and jumping at my own shadow.

Around five o'clock the birds started cheeping. Never had I heard a more soothing sound. The dawn broke soon after that, the half-light seeping in through the uncovered window in the kitchen, where I happened to be at the time. Feeling better, I went back to bed and fell asleep quite quickly. Only to be woken up a few hours later by the sound of my mobile ringing. It was Dave, calling to remind me that I was supposed to have opened the store that morning. He had turned up for his shift expecting to find me and had had to open up himself. Several customers had already called up to complain about the store being closed and he was not happy to have spent the first hour of his shift apologising to people for my oversight. I was annoyed with him. He seemed to have forgotten the night before and the fact that it may have had something to do with my no-show. But then that was one of the things I liked about him: he was conscientious almost to a fault.

In all the time he and I worked together I couldn't remember him ever missing a shift. 'Sorry, homes,' I said, 'completely forgot.' He accepted my apology, but added sarcastically, 'I don't know if you're trying to make me sack you, but if you are, it won't happen. I expect you to work out your two weeks' notice. And get your arse here asap, will ya? The price changes happen today remember? We've got a lot of stickering to do, my friend. And in case you'd forgotten, the ice-cream gets delivered later on and there's no way I'm putting that shit away by myself. And don't even get me started on the cleaning. You seen the state of the place recently? In fact, when was the last time you got the hoover out, Simon?' I was about to say that I never did the hoovering as no-one else seemed to bother, but then I remembered that he was only joking and that I would soon be out of there. And so I allowed him to prattle on till finally I could take no more and said, 'OK, OK, don't get your G-string in a twist. I'll be there shortly.'

* * *

'So, tell me, how much d'you need to buy Trevor out?' Rhona bit her lip and looked at me uncertainly. Despite all her questions, I hadn't told her how much I was getting for my story because as far as I was concerned the sum was obscene and I was embarrassed to mention it. 'At least ten g's,' she said, her voice heavy with regret, 'but I'll take whatever you can afford. Even a quarter of that would help, actually.'

We were sitting on the sofa-bed in the extension, sharing a beer, the door open to let in a bit of the cool evening air. Her back garden, a narrow patch of grass dotted with clumps of dandelion, was alive with bugs. I had not long finished my shift and had brought round a couple of games for her – the latest versions of *Assassin's Creed* and *Modern Warfare* – which were still lying on the table where I had put them, still in their Blockbuster plastic bag.

'You can have the ten grand.'

Her eyes widened. 'Come again?'

I took a sip from my glass of ice-cold beer.

'I said you can have the money. Just as soon as I have it, of course.'

She stood up and came over and sat on my lap. As usual in that situation I became nervous.

Unlike Rhona, I was always worried about being interrupted by Sky, who at that moment was in the front

50

room watching *Eastenders* with the volume turned up way too high. I kept looking over my shoulder expecting her to appear. I had never liked showing affection to Rhona in front of her. The funny thing was Sky didn't mind, and certainly Rhona didn't, but all the same there was something about it that made me uneasy. She kissed me and said, 'You really mean it?' I held her round her waist, shifting her weight slightly so as not to impede my hard on. 'Of course I mean it, woman. And I was thinking, if it's alright with you that is, I was thinking of putting a little something into an account for Sky: you know, for when she turns eighteen? What do you reckon?' Rhona smiled, put her arms around my neck and kissed me again. I was getting more and more turned on. But for the thought of Sky, I would have taken her right there in the extension. At last we broke for some air and Rhona said, 'Now come on, Simon. All joking aside. Exactly how much is the paper paying you?' I laughed. 'That's for me to know and for you to find out.'

* * *

The photographer showed up equipped with everything except his manners. His sullen, can't-be-arsed attitude was the complete opposite of Susie Lowencrantz's hard-nosed professionalism. I had the feeling he thought he was some kind of artist who should be taking pictures for an exhibition rather than for newspapers. Long-haired, pale-faced and hollow-cheeked, he was wearing a washed-out black T-shirt, black skinny jeans and a pair of battered red Converse. But for his age – he must have been fifty if he was a day – he could have passed for an indie-rocker. I made it clear to him right from the off that I wouldn't pose for any pictures that made me look like a thug. 'And how do you propose we do that?' he asked, which was either an innocent remark or an attempt to insult me.

I decided to give him the benefit of the doubt. 'Well, for one thing, I intend to be smiling in all the photos. So if that's a problem for you, we might as well end this right now.'

He didn't have a problem with me smiling, but warned that it might not reflect the serious nature of the article. I said, 'That's not my problem,' and then quickly added, 'and another thing, no pictures of me standing next to run-down council estates or walls covered in graffiti. In fact, I think we should get out into the countryside for the shoot. We could take your car.'

I was really laying down the law, and I could see that he was having to grit his teeth to avoid giving me a piece of his mind, but in the end he agreed to my suggestion. Once we were out in the countryside, and once we had agreed on a location – a shaded patch of grass beside a stream filled with shiny pebbles – we both relaxed and I started to enjoy the photo-shoot. I felt like quite the star. At one point an elderly couple driving by stopped their car in the middle of the road to see what was happening. 'Who's this black man having his photo taken? Must be somebody.' It amused me to see their puzzled faces. At that moment I believe I finally understood the attraction of fame. I had to admit it to myself, I was starting to enjoy all the attention.

* * *

When I received my cheque, minus Richard's commission, I stared at it for ages. It had my name on it, yet I couldn't escape the feeling it had been sent to me by mistake. As if I feared getting a call to confirm the mistake, I hot-footed it into town to deposit the money into my near-empty Barclays account. When I approached her cubicle, Maureen, the bespectacled, middle-aged cashier, said, 'Morning, Mr Weekes. How are you today?'

I did my best not to stare at her ample bosom. 'I'm good, thanks. And you?'

'Mustn't grumble, as they say.'

I handed her the cheque. When she saw the amount her eyes widened momentarily, but she quickly composed herself, processed the cheque, stamped it, filed it away, gave me a receipt and said, 'Now don't you go spending that all at once.' She winked at me over her quarter-moon glasses then looked past me to the next person in the queue. 'Can I help?'

I walked towards the exit and was about to step outside when, from a side door, I saw the branch manager, Geoff Walker, approaching me fast. I stopped to wait for him. The bank had no air-conditioning and it was a hot late summer's afternoon, yet Walker was wearing a creased, grey, pin-stripe suit and a tie. The heat had turned his face a crab-like pink and there was a bead of sweat on his tall forehead and another across his thin top lip. He extended his bony, blue-veined hand and said, 'Mr Weekes, good to see you.' I shook his hand. It was sweaty. 'How's it going?' I asked. He shrugged and had a quick look around, as though fearing he might be overheard.

'Got a few minutes?' I didn't, as it happened. I had a train to catch. 'Not really. Why?' He lowered his voice conspiratorially and said, 'Well, when you have a bit of time pop in and see me. I'd like to talk to you about some of the ways you might like to invest your money. In all conscience, I couldn't allow you to have such a sum sitting in a current account doing nothing for you.' I thought that was priceless. 'You mean doing nothing for the bank.' He flushed even redder than before. He was about to say something, no doubt in his defence, but I interrupted him. 'Look, I'm off to London just now, be gone a couple of days, max. I promise I'll drop by when I get back.' He flashed me a crooked grin, we shook hands again and I turned and walked away. When I got outside, I looked back to make sure Walker wasn't watching then wiped my palm on my jeans.

The unreliability of my old Golf, coupled with the hassle of having to find somewhere to park, put me off the idea of driving to London. That was half the reason. The other half was my desire to conquer my fear of getting on a train again. And it was very much fear. Just the idea of it set my heart racing. The train journey to London was going to be bad enough, but how would I feel about getting the tube from Kings Cross to Ladbroke Grove?

As it turned out, the train ride to London was not as bad as I had feared. The views into London – flat green fields, undulating hills, big blue skies – worked on me like a balm. After a panicky quarter of an hour or so, I managed to relax and passed the four-hour trip in contemplation of what it would be like to spend a bit of time with my brother. I missed him. I needed him like never before. With our parents now out of the picture, he was all the family I had left.

If the train ride into London had been manageable, then getting on the tube proved to be a severe test of my mettle. As I stood at the top of the escalator on my way to catch the Hammersmith and City Line I was not just afraid, I was terrified. People pushed past me, giving me dirty looks. On the journey into London I had been steeling myself for the moment; now that it had arrived, I didn't think I could go through with it. I tried to think rationally. Nothing was going to happen to me. I wasn't going to be blown up. And yet my knees were shaking. I dilly-dallied like this for several minutes until, suddenly, I found myself being swept on to the escalator by a huge throng of commuters.

Instinctively I stepped to the right to avoid the moving traffic, gripping the handrail for all I was worth. I took several deep breaths to try to open my lungs, but so hot and acrid was the air that I started to hyperventilate. The distance from top to bottom couldn't have been more than thirty metres but if felt twice as long. To ease my anxiety, I glanced occasionally at the ads on the wall, but all the while I was conscious of going down, ever down, as if I was heading into the very depths of hell.

As soon as I reached the bottom I jumped off the escalator and stood to one side to avoid being stampeded, still unsure whether to continue my journey. With my back against the wall, I felt a blast of cool air caused by a train entering a tunnel. I was glad for it. It helped my breathing a little, even if it did nothing for my shakes. I started talking to myself: 'If you can make it on to the train, you'll be fine.' I set out along the tunnel towards the platform. By the time I got there I was a bundle of nerves. I slumped down on the first bench I came across, practically falling into the lap of a young American couple who, not surprisingly, immediately stood up and moved some distance away from me. From the electronic timetable I saw that my train wasn't due for another seven minutes. In my current state that was an eternity. I gritted my teeth, determined not to buckle under the pressure.

Everywhere I looked I noticed people in full possession of themselves: laughing and joking, reading the Metro, listening to their iPods, gazing absently at the ads on the tunnel wall. A couple of kids were pointing at the tracks and giggling, maybe at the sight of mice. To my eyes, the people didn't seem to have a care in the world. Their composure seemed to be mocking me. I couldn't be sure how I appeared to them, but I guessed from their indifference that I seemed normal. It was a small comfort to know that I didn't look unhinged, even if that's how I felt. Even the American couple, who had initially kept a wary eye on me, were now ignoring me. With these thoughts in mind, my breathing evened out a bit. I was calming down. But the instant I saw my train approaching I got an attack of prickly heat and my throat became excessively dry.

Slowly, the train came squealing to a standstill. The noise was so distressing I involuntarily covered my ears. As usual, the commuters made a mad dash towards the edge of the platform and started bunching up on either side of the electronic doors. I remained rooted to the bench. I wasn't sure if I had it in me to get up. My legs felt numb. The train finally spat out the exiting passengers and those boarding scrambled forward to replace them. At the last second I stood up and shuffled the short distance from the bench to the train. I left it so late that the closing doors almost squashed me. But that was the least of my problems. There was not a seat to be had anywhere, so I had to support myself with a combination of my rubbery legs and the overhead railing. When the train suddenly lurched into motion, a surge of bile rose from my stomach up to my throat. I had to swallow hard to stop myself from vomiting.

For the next few stops I clung onto the overhead railing and planted my legs as firmly as I could to avoid too much swaying about. With so many people crammed into the carriage and with the ever-changing motion of the train as it wound its way through the tunnel, this was no easy feat. Waves of nausea washed over me. Having a seat would have helped, but I was never quick enough or in the right position to grab any free ones. And then things took a significant turn for the worse. Due to what the driver announced as 'signal problems up ahead', the train stopped in a tunnel. At this point I felt myself swoon. Convinced I was on the point of collapse, I took the desperate measure of sitting down on the carriage floor. Squeezing myself between the throng, I positioned myself so that my back was flat against the Perspex partition and then slid down on to the floor, drawing my knees up to my stomach to make myself as small as possible.

I drew a lot of stares from those around me, scornful, judgemental, even hateful stares, but by then I was beyond caring. Clutching my small backpack containing a change of clothes and a few toiletries, I sat and waited for the train to get going again. Looking around, I had the sudden macabre thought that if an explosion were to go off just then, dozens of people would be blown to smithereens, and that thought prompted me to examine some of the faces of the people standing near me. I don't know what I was looking for, some sense of who they were I guess. Maybe I was trying to connect with them on some level, trying to get past the barriers, barriers that rarely come down except in a crisis or a catastrophe. When I thought back to the bombing and how close I had felt to all the survivors and even to the dead, I could hardly believe that only a few weeks later I was sitting on the floor of a tube train, feeling scared out of my mind, hoping to be ignored.

In the middle of having these thoughts, the visions began, flashing before my eyes in rapid succession. Once again I saw the room, that dark, depressing room where it all took place. I saw Mitch, his eyes wild with rage, his knife drawn, yearning to tear me apart for my betrayal but afraid of the gun in my hand. I saw Benjy, looking lost, his loyalty hopelessly divided between his two best friends. And I saw myself, ordering them around, high on coke and power, full of self-loathing and the desire to blow my own brains out. In between the visions I struggled to get perspective on my surroundings. My spatial awareness became shot. I couldn't work out where I stood, or rather sat, in relation to the other passengers. At first the man standing in front of me seemed to be within touching distance, and then he appeared to be out of reach. Likewise the little girl holding his hand. I almost reached out my hand to test the distance between us. But I didn't. I didn't because I was desperate not to appear crazy or threatening. I fought like the devil to keep a lid on things.

I felt like crying out, but my pride wouldn't allow to me to behave that way in front of all those hard-faced Londoners. I didn't want to give them the added satisfaction. To them I must have seemed like a nutter sitting there on the floor, but

I didn't want them to start treating me like one by moving away from me. Normally on a tube I wanted as much space for myself as I could get, but in that situation, the closer I was to my fellow passengers the better I felt. It meant I was normal. It meant I was sane. Some of them were clearly scared of me. I couldn't say I blamed them. They didn't recognise me, they didn't know who I was or what I'd done, and even if they did, it wouldn't have mattered. It hadn't been two months since the bombings, they were still on edge, still wary of anything or anyone that looked suspicious or out of the ordinary. I felt the same. As soon as I stepped into that carriage I started looking around for anyone, man or woman, with a backpack. Who was to say there wasn't another suicide bomber lurking in the carriage? For all those passengers knew, I could be one. I wasn't Asian, I didn't fit the racial profile, but neither had Germaine Lindsay, a black guy like myself who'd blown up the train at Kings Cross.

At last the driver apologised for the delay. Soon after that the train hissed and sighed and juddered to a start. Within a few minutes the visions ceased and the agitation I had been feeling started to wane. Just to be on the move again had given me a shot in the arm. But still I remained on the floor. With each successive stop the train became emptier and more and more seats became available, but I remained on the floor. When it pulled into Edgware Road, I became so scared I couldn't even open my eyes but there was no escape from the memory. I was right back there. I saw it all. The train pulling into the station. The doors opening and staying open. The people getting on, the others getting off and crossing to the platform opposite, but mostly I saw the faces of the people who'd been in the carriage with me that day, none clearer than Mohammad Sidique Khan. As soon as I pictured his face I opened my eyes, half expecting to see him sitting in front of me, but the first thing I saw was a pigeon. It had wandered in and was walking around looking for food. Outside the carriage, people were milling about, looking up at the notice board, checking which train they needed to catch and on which platform. I sat on the floor and watched them, impatient for the train to get going, more impatient than I'd been on the day of the bombing. The doors seemed to take an age to close. Finally, I heard, 'This train is now ready to depart. Please stand clear of the closing doors.' The doors slid together, trapping the pigeon. It didn't seem to mind. It waddled along the carriage in my direction, its head bobbing up and down and jerking back and forth. It didn't seem to notice me and when it did, it shot me a quick sideways glance then continued on its way, pecking the ground as it went. It came so close to me I couldn't fail to notice that one of its claws had been damaged, was essentially a stump, and that its eyes were very milky.

As the train pulled out of the station, I began to wonder whether I would be able to get off at my stop, which was drawing ever closer. When it left Westbourne Park and began its approach into Ladbroke Grove, I realised I had to do something or face the very real prospect of riding it all the way to Hammersmith. I had to act. Turning to a black teenager who was sitting nearby, I said, 'You couldn't gimme a hand, could you? I'm having a bit of trouble standing up.' At first he looked at me as if I was a turd, but then he began scrutinising my face more closely and I saw the light of recognition appear in his eyes.

'Wait a sec, ain't you that brer from the papers…the one who saved all them…'

I nodded and he immediately leaped forward and helped me to my feet.

'Rah! What happened to you?'

'It's long,' I replied. He tried to usher me into a seat but I told him I was getting off at the next stop. When he said, 'Me too,' it was music to my ears.

He held on to me till the train pulled into the station and then helped me first onto the platform, and then out of the station altogether. Before we parted company he said, 'You gonna be alright from here, blood?' I nodded, we touched fists and he bounced off down the road. I had been leaning against the station wall and when I tried to walk my legs wobbled, but they didn't give out. More staggering than walking, I made my way to my brother's flat, cursing the fact that he had, for what he had described to me as 'a change of scenery', decided to move all the way from Hackney to Ladbroke Grove.

Before I went to see him, I had confided in Theodore about my anxiety over travelling on trains again. Not only had he said, 'You gotta get back on the horse, bro,' he'd been most insistent on the point. Yet when he opened his front door and saw me, his first words were, 'Maybe you should have driven after all. You look terrible.' It was intended as a piece of gallows humour. He had no way of knowing what I had just been through, but even so I resented his blasé remark.

Theodore had come a long way since the days when he and his gang went around brandishing sawn-off shotguns and demanding money with menaces. In many ways he had led a very charmed life. For all the crimes he had committed he had never spent so much as a day in prison. Then there was the small matter of him cheating death. I once told him that he was a 'jammy git' and he replied that luck had nothing to do with it, that it was all God's work. When I asked him if it was God's work that he had been stabbed to within an inch of his life, he said, 'The Lord works in mysterious ways.' That was him. Everything he said or did was shaped by his belief in God. He once showed me something he wrote for his church pamphlet, which was a good example of how steeped he had become in his faith.

The most important thing for me now is to live a pure life. To strive for anything less would be unworthy of me. From now on I aim to be righteous in all my thoughts and actions. The cynic would say, "Don't be a fool, Theodore. God doesn't expect you to be perfect," and straightaway I would say, "Maybe not, but He loves a trier." And that is now my purpose in life. I want to please God. He has given me a second chance and I want to show Him that I'm worthy of it. To do that I must first accept that I exist only through His grace and then live my life in strict accordance with His laws.

He was a Christian. Pure and simple. He believed, with all his heart, that Jesus was the son of God and that He had been sent from heaven to redeem us from our sins. On that his position was fixed and I never once saw him deviate from it. His faith was strong and complete and I have to say that I envied what he got from it, the security it gave him. If we're all searching for something to believe in, something to give meaning to our lives, his search had ended. As a result, he was the most peaceful person I knew. He wasn't constantly straining at the leash like I was. He had none of my cravings. If he hungered after anything it was to have a closer relationship with God. He certainly didn't feel any guilt or shame about the misdeeds of his youth, unlike me. He had, he said, been to the Holy River and washed himself clean. What did he care about being judged by people when the Supreme Judge had absolved him of his sins? From what he had led me to believe, he had but two bugbears. He was slightly dissatisfied with his job – he worked for a big DIY store – and was frustrated by his inability to find the right woman to settle down with. In that sense he was not unlike millions of other people, but he was unusual in that he never complained, he never whined, he didn't believe in shaking his fist at the world. 'I bring everything to the Lord in prayer.'

I had made up my mind not to burden Theodore with my ongoing problems. For the first evening I spent with him I kept to that promise, we talked about everything except the bombing, but I couldn't keep it up and by the end of the second day I had confided in him about the visions and how badly they had been affecting me. 'There are people you can see for that, you know? Counsellors and such. I'm sure you can even get that kind of thing on the NHS.' I also told him that I was fed up with leading a double life and that I regularly felt the urge to unburden myself of my ugly secret.

'Confession is a part of healing, Simon. If you don't confess what you've done, if you don't own up to it, you'll never be free of it.'

'Yeah, but who do I confess to?'

'To God.'

'But I don't believe in God.'

'Then you really are lost.'

He then ordered me to bow my head and, as he always did whenever I went to see him, he offered up a prayer for my salvation.

Before I left him, I asked Theodore whether he needed money for anything. 'I got quite a bit for the article, so I was wondering…' I had barely finished my sentence before he started shaking his head. 'I'm good. But I know a couple of people who could always use a few extra quid. You could send them a cheque. Better still, why not take it to them in person?'

It was a familiar tactic. He wasted no opportunity to try to push me in the direction of our parents. He was never so direct as to say, 'Things are not right between you and those guys, they haven't been for a long time now, do something about it, Simon,' but he would allude to it. He spoke regularly to Mum and Dad on the phone and would call me immediately afterwards to pass on their regards, even if they hadn't asked him to. More recently he had been trying to get me to go to Jamaica. 'You should get out there. I'm sure it would do you good to spend some time with the folks.' The child in me, the one who liked to do things his own way and in his own time, always resisted these promptings, but underneath I was happy that Theodore took the trouble, for no matter the distance between us, no matter that I hadn't seen them in years, at the end of the day I had a responsibility to my parents. If I sometimes forgot that then Theodore was always on hand to remind me.

To spare myself the ordeal of travelling back to Kings Cross on the tube, I opted to take a mini-cab to Kings Cross station. In the cab on the way, and then later on the overland train, I mulled over some of the things I had discussed with Theodore. By advising me to talk to someone about the visions I was having he had given me much food for thought. Counselling. I couldn't see the harm in it. I had to do something and that seemed as good a thing to try as any. What did I have to lose? Theodore had seemed certain that I stood to gain by it.

He had also been pretty convinced that I would benefit from spending a bit of time with the folks. I felt the same. Over the years I had become virtually estranged from my parents, but since the bombing their pull had been getting stronger and stronger. It wasn't going to be easy, but I had to try to find a way to re-connect with them, and as a matter of urgency. They were not getting any younger. The fact of their mortality was something I could no longer turn away from. It was time I went to see them. The only problem was I had no particular desire to go to Jamaica. I had no interest in the place. In contrast to Theodore, I didn't regard going there as some kind of pilgrimage that had to be undertaken before I kicked the bucket.

I had always been uneasy about my Jamaican heritage. As a child I resented it. I wanted to be English. That's how I saw myself and that's how I wanted others to see me. For my parents, the matter was a bit more complicated. They encouraged us, the younger generation, in our Englishness, but at the same time wanted us to acknowledge our Jamaican side and were scandalised if ever we tried to deny it. This was something we regularly did, especially at school, where a lot of the white kids would tease us and call us racist names and tell us to go back to our country. As we got older we began to realise that no matter how hard we tried, in the eyes of certain sections of white society we were not and never would be English. I couldn't speak for Theodore, but it made me sad to be denied something I felt belonged to me. But I wasn't going to beg. If I wasn't welcome in the club then it couldn't be worth joining. And so, feeling rejected, and with my tail between my legs, I turned towards the very thing I'd been running from, towards Jamaica. The music, the food, the lingo, the attitude: I embraced it all. And yet for all that there remained the issue of authenticity. When it came right down to it, I was not the real deal. I was not born in Jamaica. I had never even visited the place. So how could I call myself a Jamaican? In the end I came to accept that I was neither one thing nor the other, neither English nor Jamaican. I was something in between, something vague and indefinable. I had accepted it but I wasn't happy. I doubted I ever would be.

* * *

The guys at Blockbuster had left the choice of pub up to me. My leaving do, my privilege. To avoid any chance of bumping into Trevor, I chose a bright, noisy sports bar in the centre of town. The evening was a success, meaning there was a lot of alcohol and a lot of juvenile behaviour. And the whole thing only set me back about two hundred quid. When I got home I could hardly get my key in the door and no sooner was I inside than I sparked out, fully dressed, on the sofa. I slept fitfully, disturbed by bad dreams. In one I was drowning and in another I was being dragged, screaming, towards a guillotine with a masked executioner standing beside it. I woke up around noon the next day with a parched throat, a pounding head and a feeling of having been in the wars, yet grateful that I had at least been spared my usual nightmares. I staggered to the bathroom to empty my bursting bladder and when I saw myself in the mirror I had quite a shock. Someone, probably Dave, had written the word 'Fanny' in black marker on my forehead.

About an hour later, with a cup of instant coffee and some toast inside me, I went out and bought a copy of the *Sunday Mirror*. Rhona had invited me round for lunch and had asked me to bring along a copy of the paper so we could look over the article together, but I couldn't wait and ended up reading it on the pavement outside Len's newsagents. Several people passed me on the way into the shop, and I heard at least one of them say, 'Afternoon', but I was so engrossed in the paper that I didn't even lift my head, much less return the greeting.

The interview came with a lot of illustrations. In the absence of photos, a sketch artist had been hired to try to capture the scenes of carnage as I had described them. The busted up carriage and the expressions on the faces of the survivors were skilfully, if melodramatically, done. I wasn't sure why, but the images seemed the more effective, the more powerful, for being drawn. As to the article itself, Susie Lowencrantz really went to town. If she had been a bit restrained in the first part of the piece, if she had kept herself in check whilst describing the less eventful build up to the bombing, by the midpoint her voice was in full, exaggerated cry. No sentence was complete without an 'incredible', or an 'astonishing' and my efforts to help Latonya were described as 'superhuman'. Time and again she would bring a particular piece of action to the point of climax, then drag the reader off on some tangent or other, all in the name of building tension. It was hard to tell if this was tabloid journalism at its gripping, suspenseful best, or sensationalist, manipulative worst. Certainly I was hooked from the first sentence to the last, but whether that was down to good writing, or my own vanity, I just wasn't sure.

Rhona didn't have much to say about the article except, 'I found it a bit full on, to be honest.' When I asked her to explain, she said, 'It just seemed a bit too much all that stuff about people having their arms and legs blown off.' She turned up her nose as though she had smelt a dead rat. I became defensive. 'They wanted details, I gave them details. That's what they were paying me for.' Sensing I was spoiling for an argument, she deflected the blame on to the paper. 'Honestly, that *Sunday Mirror*'s a blooming rag. Hungry?' I nodded and she went off to the kitchen.

While she was out of the room I thought about her reaction to the article, which had been out-and-out squeamish. The irony of this was not lost on me, even if it was on her. She was obsessed with ultra-violent computer games, but went white at the thought of real violence. I saw the relish she took in hacking the heads off her virtual enemies, in gutting them like fish, but if she saw a couple of guys scuffling in the street she had to look away. I once invited her to a football match but she turned me down because she thought there was too much fighting amongst the fans. I tried to convince her that those days were over, that the violence in English football was now mostly conducted away from the stadiums, but she wouldn't have it. 'I'm not interested, Simon. I want nothing to do with those chavvy yobs.'

Later that week, as a thank-you for all the support they had shown me since the bombing, I offered to take Rhona and Sky out for a meal. I almost changed my mind as it took us ages to decide where to go. Rhona fancied an Indian, Sky was up for an Italian, while I wanted a Chinese. We spent a long time arguing the merits of each country's cuisine, as though we were trying to prove a case in court, but in the end none of us got our way. We went to an Angus Steak House instead. Sky invited her boyfriend, Euan, a self-styled EMO with lank, greasy hair and a face full of spots. Throughout dinner he must have spoken two words.

On our way back from the restaurant, while he and Sky were walking hand-in-hand in front of us, I said to Rhona, 'What's she doing with that boy? He's proper weird.'

Rhona stifled a giggle and said, 'What can I say? She loves him.'

I snorted. 'Love. She's sixteen, for crying out loud.'

That stopped Rhona in her tracks. 'You old cynic, you. You mean you don't believe in young love?'

I didn't answer but later that night, in bed, with Rhona asleep beside me, I thought some more about her question. 'You don't believe in young love?' This led me to thinking about her and Trevor. She had once told me that their marriage had been made in heaven. Childhood sweethearts who wed at eighteen, they were seen by their friends and family as the golden couple. But according to Rhona, it was a façade. Almost from day one she realised she'd made a mistake in getting married. 'I was young and in love. It seemed like the

normal thing to do. After two years I was bored out my mind.'
She was 'young and in love'. Sky was 'young and in love', but
the question was: would the daughter make the same mistake
as the mother? Would Sky get married too soon, have a child
while she herself was barely out of nappies, then repent at her
leisure? I couldn't see it. She had a lot of her mother in her,
but Sky just didn't strike me as the type to throw her life away.

Maybe I was projecting my own failed hopes and
ambitions on to her, or maybe I just had too many depressing
memories of teenage mothers from my childhood. Like my
old girlfriend, Beverly, for example. She'd had a child while
still at school and her life was over before it had begun.
I didn't want that for Sky. I was horrified at the thought
that she wouldn't go on to live a full life. I wanted her to
travel, to have adventures, to leave her mark on the world.
What I did not want was to see her get hitched to the first
spotty teenager that happened along and settle down – in
Duddenham of all places – to a life of drudge. For a girl as
intelligent as her, for a girl with her spark, that would have
been nothing short of a tragedy. And it would have been all
the more tragic if Rhona had sat idly by and let it happen,
which she seemed hell-bent on doing.

* * *

Now that I wasn't working, I had more time on my hands
than I knew what to do with. This gave me ample opportunity
to think. On the whole I thought things were going well.
Having survived the bombing without a scratch, what did I
really have to complain about? I had mental wounds, it's true,

but they would heal. Before releasing me from hospital on the day of the bombing, the doctor had warned me that, in the weeks to come, I may well experience symptoms consistent with post-traumatic stress. 'You'll have nightmares, that's almost a given, and you'll sometimes feel anxious, especially in public, and that may lead to full-blown panic attacks. All perfectly normal. Your brain has received a massive shock. It will recover in time. But you must look after yourself. For the next few months I want you to take it easy, get plenty of rest and don't do anything too stressful.'

I'd had my fair share of nightmares and anxiety attacks, as well as sudden fits of rage and insomnia, but it could have been so much worse. Unlike some survivors, I had yet to experience the intense guilt at being alive, I hadn't suffered impotence or a drop in my libido, I hadn't lost my hair, I wasn't crying all the time, I hadn't taken to my bed and refused to have any contact with my friends and family, I knew nothing of the compulsion to visit the relatives of the deceased, I hadn't fallen victim to claustrophobia, I didn't hate all Muslims or even some of them, and I had no desire to find a quiet place in the world where I could see out the rest of my days in peace and security. I was doing alright.

It was in this state of optimism that I decided to write to my parents. I rarely called them in Jamaica because I always struggled to get through. It seemed incredible to me that in the twenty-first-century their village was still not hooked up to the island's national phone grid. They had a shared mobile – their first, bought specifically so Theodore and I could keep in touch – but it was very expensive to call and had a crap reception. I hardly ever got a proper connection, and when I did the line would be so faint and crackly as to make conversation virtually impossible. None of this seemed to bother Theodore. What mattered to him was the frequency of the conversations he had with our parents, not the quality. For me it was the other way around. If I took the time to contact mum and dad it was because I really wanted to talk to them, because I actually had stuff to say to them. That's why I preferred writing. Old fashioned it may have been, but it was the ideal way for me to express myself to them without interruption.

At a dozen pages, the letter was very long. I hadn't intended it that way, but once I began writing, thoughts and sentiments just flowed and flowed. I imagined my parents were going to be embarrassed by my emotional outpourings, and I knew for certain that their return letter would be as brief as mine had been long-winded, but frankly I didn't care. In the end, writing to my parents was just another way of communicating with myself. With the letter written and ready to go, I decided I would kill two birds with one stone and make arrangements with my bank to transfer some money into my parents' account in Jamaica. The idea was for them to receive the letter and the money at roughly the same time.

On my way to the bank I popped into Len's newsagents to buy an envelope and some stamps. I didn't want to trek all the way into town to queue up at the post-office. It was just after ten on a Monday morning and the place would have been thick with OAPs cashing their pensions. As I entered his shop I said to Len, 'Stick 'em up!' It was my usual greeting, but Len didn't give his usual response. Instead of saying, 'I can't, I'm too old,' he said, 'Oh. Simon. I didn't think...sorry...

you surprised me…I was just…' He did something under the counter with his hands, something furtive. He seemed very nervous and for some reason couldn't look me in the eye. 'Everything OK, Len?' At that point he stopped fidgeting and our eyes finally made four. He said, 'You don't know, do you?' I studied his face. His expression couldn't have been more grave. 'Know what, Len?' From under the counter he brought out a copy of *The Sun*, which he had obviously been reading. He put it down on the counter so that I could get a good view of the front page. And there it was: *BOMB HERO IS CONVICTED GANG RAPIST.*

Part Two

These days Hackney is one of London's most gentrified boroughs, but when I was growing up there in the seventies and eighties, it was the very definition of the shitty, inner-city ghetto. My family lived in a street where every other building was either derelict or unfit for human habitation. Our own house, a four-storey, rat-infested, post-war terrace gave us no protection in winter. Without central heating, the rooms may as well have been freezers. I had to sleep wearing layers of clothing, beneath layers of blankets. We had electric and Calor gas heaters, but these were so expensive to run our parents had to ration how we used them. That only left paraffin heaters, which, though cheaper to run, were dangerous and ineffective, so ineffective that I regularly got chilblains on my fingers and toes from all the hours I spent huddled over them trying to warm up.

During one particularly grim winter, I went to bed wearing a bobble hat. From the top-bunk, Theodore started teasing me and we ended up fighting. Attracted to the commotion, Dad came to investigate and had to separate us. When he heard what we'd been fighting about, he surprised me by bawling out Theodore. 'That is anything to tease you brother about? Cold is no joke boy.' He then told a story about his first winter in London in 1963, which he called the 'The Big Freeze'. Straight off the boat train from Jamaica, he'd been so cold he'd caught pneumonia. The story explained why he and Mum were constantly at loggerheads with our landlord, Mr. Beresford, a curmudgeonly Barbadian who lived in relative luxury in the basement of our house while we lived in squalor on the two upper floors. Fortunately my parents were more than a match for him. Aware of their legal rights, they used the courts to force him to make improvements to the house, but in the end they got fed up with all the aggravation and started harassing the council to find us a better place to live. It took years but eventually they moved us into a recently-vacated two-bedroom flat. Though cleaner, warmer and more spacious, it had the drawback of being in a very rough area. Relieved just to have new accommodation, and at a much lower rent, and with central heating throughout, my parents either didn't see or deliberately chose to ignore the fact that our neighbours now included pimps, prostitutes and drug dealers.

* * *

As with most immigrants who came over from the Caribbean in the fifties and sixties, my parents seemed to do nothing but work. Dad, a bus driver, regularly took on extra shifts. It was not uncommon for him to be on the job till well after eleven at night. Mum worked as a cleaner at Hackney Hospital, a job that kept her on her feet all day, swelling her ankles and leaving her exhausted. But no matter how tired she'd be, she'd always cook dinner when she came home. After we'd eaten, she'd issue instructions for me to wash up and for Theodore to put the Hoover round and take out the rubbish and the empty milk bottles. She would then put her feet up on her favourite pouf, letting out a sigh of pleasure at being able to rest her swollen ankles, reach for her packet of Rothmans and switch on our Rediffusion TV with the remote. After one cigarette she'd be snoring, the cigarette having burned down in the ashtray. We usually had to wake her up for the noise, at which point she'd say, 'I going for a lie down'. I always looked forward to this moment because I knew she was never coming back.

I'd spend the rest of the evening in front of the TV, pigging out on post-watershed classics like *Starsky and Hutch*, *The Rockford Files* and *Kojak*. Theodore would take to the streets, often staying out till the small hours when he knew Mum and Dad were asleep. He made me his accomplice, bribing me with alcohol and cigarettes and even the odd bit of weed. Our bedroom was at the back of the house, so he'd whistle up and I'd sneak downstairs and let him in. Sometimes I'd sleep through his call and he'd have to throw stones against the window. One night he cracked the window and we had to invent a story about knocking into it by accident. On another night Mum woke up to go to the toilet and caught us creeping up the stairs. We swore to her that it was a one-off but she didn't believe us. When she came home from work that evening she kept her promise and beat us: me first, then Theodore. By the time Dad came home we were already in bed but still he came into our room and warned us about our future conduct. He was especially angry with Theodore. 'Either abide by what we tell you or haul your tail out of this house.' That situation came to pass sooner than any of us expected. Not long after this Theodore got arrested for shoplifting. He was let off with a caution but still Mum beat him with such viciousness that I started crying from fear. I had never seen her like that, wild, with a demented look in her eye, as if she was possessed, and it was certainly not a pretty sight to see my older brother, who I adored, reduced to a blubbering wreck.

But at least it wasn't Dad's job to dish out the punishment. He was a huge, serious man, over six feet tall with hands the size of baseball mittens. One blow from him and Theodore might have ended up in hospital. As it turned out, Dad couldn't forgive Theodore and started acting as if he didn't exist. The feeling was mutual. For weeks they didn't speak to each other. Mum tried hard to patch things up between them but failed. Matters came to a head when the police called to say that Theodore had been arrested for 'going equipped'. He'd been caught with a hole-punch, the car thief's main tool.

I was standing next to Mum when she took the call. She broke down and sobbed, wondering aloud about what she had done to deserve such a wayward child. Between sniffles, she called Dad at work. Theodore had no means of getting home so Dad had to clock off early to go and pick him up from Lewisham police station. When they got in, Dad marched him to our room and stood over him while he packed up his few possessions. I begged Dad to reconsider, Mum did too, but he had made up his mind. It wouldn't have mattered anyway. Theodore wanted to go. When he had all his things together, Dad, who hadn't said a word throughout, escorted him to the front door.

When Theodore left I was devastated. All of a sudden I was alone. Without his presence, our room felt too big, the space seemed too much for me. As a way to remain close to him, I started sleeping on his bunk and never went back to mine. Nights were the worst. We used to laugh and joke our way to sleep; now I had nothing but my thoughts, which jumped about and kept me awake till all hours. Weekends were not much better. On Saturday mornings, with Dad still in bed and after Mum had gone shopping in Ridley Road Market, I had to watch *Football Focus* by myself, debating the topics in my head where I used to debate them with Theodore. Sundays meant church, but without my brother at my side, cracking jokes and sending the whole thing up, I dreaded it. Other black families in our area were either Pentecostal, Seven Day Adventists or Baptists, they got to sing gospel songs and could dance in the aisles and play tambourines. We were Church of England, which meant near-empty pews, long-winded sermons, dispiriting hymns that sounded like funeral dirges and church officials so sombre they could double for morgue technicians. In winter, most of the congregation kept their coats on and scarves and you could actually hear the draughts whistling around like sprites. There were some benefits, though.

I used to be in the choir. Theodore had flatly refused to join but I did because it was a nice little earner. For every Wednesday evening that we attended choir practice, and for every Sunday that we showed up in church decked out in our black smocks and white dog collars, we were paid two pounds. We also got to ring the church bells. Climbing the ladders up to the belfry was exciting enough, but nothing compared to bell-ringing. I used to love the feeling of being hoisted into the air while clinging on to those thick, palm-burning ropes. Another perk was the all-expenses-paid annual summer holiday at Betsanger, a converted public school in the Kent countryside. I always looked forward to going there, but not half as much as my parents, who relished the opportunity to be rid of me for a whole week during the school holidays at no cost to themselves. Because I rarely left Hackney, much less London, the place seemed to me to have all the exoticism of a foreign country.

The old school building was so huge, had so many rooms, you could easily get lost in it if you weren't familiar with its layout. And the grounds were just as impressive, with enough space for a football pitch, a cricket pitch, a tennis court and an outdoor swimming pool. There was also a boxing gym, though it was rarely used except to settle disputes between us boys. I remember the year George Mensah and I squared up to each other in the ring. Mensah was an out-and-out bully. We'd been caught fighting, again, and the vicar, the sadistic so-and-so, insisted that we box each other. He even positioned himself at ringside to watch the bout. Mr. Kelly, an Ulsterman, one of several church officials who always accompanied us to Betsanger and who liked to rub his whiskered chin on our faces for a laugh, volunteered to be the referee. For about five minutes, without pause, Mensah hammered away at me, cheered on by the other boys. Several of them had opened books on the outcome. Mensah was a wild thing, coming at me with tremendous speed and ferocity, throwing on average three punches for every one of mine. Most of them missed. I was very light on my feet, dancing around the ring Ali-style while trying to pick my punches, trying to conserve my energy. Later, everyone told me how much I looked the part, how stylish I had been, how I had showed up Mensah for the crude brawler that he was. Pity then that Mr. Kelly declared him the winner.

Our choir was quite the novelty within the Church of England. Due to St. Mark's catchment area, it was made up exclusively of black boys. We were once invited to sing at Canterbury Cathedral as part of its Christmas celebrations. Earlier in the day, before the service, we were taken on a tour of the cathedral's walled precincts. Everywhere we looked there was a medieval building or ruin, each one with some kind of historical significance. We visited the crypt, for example, a very spooky place dating back to the eleventh century. It was, we were told, the oldest existing part of the cathedral and it certainly felt that way. We also saw the memorial to Thomas Beckett, two swords and a broken sword point erected on a bare stone altar. We had learned all about this man from our Sunday school lessons, but to be standing on the very spot where he had been slain turned him from a famous Christian martyr into a mortal being. Nowadays, if ever I hear his name mentioned, I'm immediately transported back to that day when I stood before his shrine, staring not so much at the ancient swords, but at the eerie shadow they created against the altar. That trip to Canterbury Cathedral, with its magnificent stained-glass windows and vaulted arches, its gilt roofs, cloistered walkways and water tower, affected me profoundly. As an inner-city kid, I was blown away by the grandeur of the place, by the history, by the pageantry of the Christmas service and the sight of the Archbishop in full regalia, but most of all by the sound of the cathedral choir. I remember clearly the feeling I had as I stood listening to them, a feeling I can only describe as rapturous.

In Hackney, we choirboys had our own version of rural England. The atmosphere at St Mark's vicarage, a stone cottage built on the church grounds, was so genteel and insulated you could easily forget you were in one of the poorest parts of London and imagine yourself somewhere in the shires. We came to regard it as our own personal clubhouse. It had a billiard table, dozens of comics, a bar-football machine, Subbuteo teams with full accessories, plus any number of board games: Battleship, Buckaroo, Kerplunk!. It even had a croquet lawn out the back, pristinely manicured, but the vicar, the Reverend Donald Pateman, had forbidden us from using it for fear of the violence we might do to each other with the wooden mallets. He and his live-in housekeeper, the widowed, elderly Mrs. Smith, were posh, slightly doddering and stereotypically English. Mrs. Smith used to make sandwiches with the crusts removed.

Like a couple of missionaries, they seemed overly taken with black children and would show us special favours over the few white kids who came calling. Not that they were soft on us. They had rules and knew how to enforce them. For instance, watching TV without permission was strictly forbidden. The vicar called it the Devil's Picture Box and would only allow us to watch those programmes that he himself had carefully vetted after consulting the *Radio Times*. Anyone found guilty of breaching this rule was rewarded with six stripes of the cane. The guilty party was summoned to the vicar's panelled study, where, behind closed doors, the punishment was meted out. I remember the day George Mensah got called in. He made a detour to the bathroom and stuffed a towel into the seat of his trousers. The vicar noticed and added another couple of strokes for the attempted deception. I myself was never caned, but I would often creep to the study door and listen while the vicar did his thing, sniggering under my breath as I heard the yelps of pain.

If I wasn't at school or at church or at choir practice, I liked to hang out with my two best friends, Mitch and Benjy. As primary school kids we used to play 'had' or 'knock-down-ginger', but once we got to secondary school we left all that behind and now mostly played 'Wembley' in the middle of our street, using our jumpers and coats for goal-posts. Before he left home, Theodore would come out and join us occasionally. He was three years older than me, had his own circle of friends, but he was never so caught up in his own life that he neglected to take an interest in his little brother's. Our parents didn't force him, either, as is usually the case with older siblings; he did it because he wanted to, because, I like to think, he enjoyed my company. Now he'd gone. I was too young to appreciate this at the time, but I realised later that I went through a kind of bereavement when he left home. For weeks afterwards I refused to speak to Mum or Dad. The situation became so tense that Mum suggested I go and live with her sister, Viola, until I felt better about things and was ready to come home. I didn't go. I loved my aunt and her two daughters but had no time for her husband, Derrick. Teaching Maths at a Polytechnic had given him airs. Besides, the family lived in Croydon, which might as well have been Russia.

I continued to punish Mum and Dad by giving them the silent treatment. I hadn't seen or heard from Theodore in months, no one seemed to know where he was. I had begun to imagine all sorts of horrible scenarios. What if he was lying dead somewhere? And then, out of the blue, he stopped by one morning, dressed in some very fancy clothes and wearing a lot of jewellery on his fingers, wrists and neck. Mum had already gone to work but Dad was still at home so Theodore didn't dare knock on the door.

He met me outside and drove me to school in his metallic-green 3-series BMW. I was happy to see him but also angry that he hadn't been in touch.

'Where you been?'

'Abroad.'

'Don't lie.'

'Seriously.'

'Where abroad?'

'Spain.'

'Doing what?'

He smiled and said no more. At the school gates he gave me quite a lecture. It turned out he'd been in contact with Mum. 'You're breaking the old dear's heart, Simon. Cut her some slack. I don't give two fucks about Dad, you know that, but Mum's feeling it, bruv. She thinks you hate her.'

He lit a cigarette and wound down the window to let the smoke out. I stared at him. He had the beginnings of a beard and his voice was almost as deep as Dad's. There was also something in his eyes, a certain haunted look, as if he'd seen things not meant for boys his age. 'Just be nice to her, OK?'

It was such a surreal situation I didn't know how to respond. I had questions for him but didn't ask any as I didn't want him to think I cared: How often had he and Mum been in contact?

Had they spoken on the phone or met up or both? If they had met up, where did it happen and when and did Dad know about it? What had he been doing with himself since I last saw him? What connection did he have with Spain? Had he thought about me at all? Did he miss me as much as I missed him? The school gates were now deserted, all the children had gone in apart from a few stragglers who were being helped across the street by Millie the lollipop lady. I recognised a few faces from my year. 'When you coming round again?' I asked. He shrugged. I opened the door and got out just in time for the kids to see me. As I had hoped, they stopped to admire the car. At the last minute Theodore shouted, 'Don't forget what I said.' I ignored him and walked through the gates, answering questions as I went: Wasn't that your brother? When did he get back? His Bimmer's got petrol injection, right?

I couldn't concentrate for the rest of the morning. All I could think about was Theodore and how he much he had changed, and in such a short space of time. I didn't want to be in school that day. I wanted to be out driving with my brother, seeing the world, doing things, going to Spain. As it was I had to endure double French, which I got through by scrawling capital letters on my desk then blocking and shading them.

I didn't like my school. It was not, by any standard, a seat of academic excellence. The teachers could barely disguise their contempt for the job, while we pupils, uninspired and unmotivated, were doing nothing so much as killing time before leaving for a life of dead-end jobs or the dole. Absenteeism was a major problem, and that was just amongst the staff. Formerly the Grocer's Company, it used to be a well-respected grammar school whose old boys' included Michael Caine and Terence Stamp, no less, but by 1977, when I arrived there, it had become a comprehensive and the rot had taken hold. Renamed Hackney Fields – it overlooked a scrubby park – parents were moving out of the area to avoid sending their children there. Some time after I left it achieved nationwide notoriety when a tabloid newspaper dubbed it 'the worst school in Britain'. Shortly after that the government closed it down.

This was a culture common to virtually every inner-London state comprehensive at the time, so it's not as if I had the option to go anywhere better. By the third year I had become bored and restless and was regularly skipping classes. My end-of-term school reports began to make sorry reading. There was one in particular that had stayed with me. 'There's no doubting Simon's abilities, but he lacks application and must try harder if he hopes to fulfil his undoubted potential. He's too easily distracted.'

They were right in some cases, completely wrong in others. Yes, I found it hard to concentrate in subjects like maths, science, history, social studies, humanities, languages and geography, but would always apply myself in English and drama, especially drama. The escapism. The make-believe. In one particularly memorable class we went on a voyage into outer space. Our vessel consisted of nothing more than plastic chairs and chipboard boxes of various sizes, but to us it may as well have been the Starship Enterprise. Much of what we did was influenced by popular TV series of the day, be they sci-fi classics like *Star Trek* and *Blake's Seven* or children's favourites like *Press Gang* and *Grange Hill*. None of it felt like learning. In fact, with the classroom windows blacked out against prying eyes, it wasn't like being at school at all. In all my time at Hackney Fields, even with all the bunking off I did, I don't believe I missed a single drama lesson and in that time I appeared in three of the school's biggest productions: *Joseph and His Amazing Technicolour Dreamcoat, Oliver,* and an original, non-musical piece called *Harsh Times,* devised by ourselves, about the problems of growing up in inner-city London. I played one of the main characters, a boy from a poor family who comes to school dressed in hand-me-downs and gets teased for it. At the end of the show the cast got a standing ovation.

My other big passion was football. For four years, between the ages of eleven and fifteen, I was a permanent member of my school team. Big things were expected of me, and I expected big things of myself, but I really began to dream the day my coach told me I'd been scouted. We'd just finished playing. We'd won. I'd scored. Even now, so many years later, I can still remember the jubilation I felt when the final whistle went. Things got even better when, as we were leaving the pitch, our heads steaming in the winter chill, Mr. Ludlow came alongside me and whispered, 'Was a scout here today. Leyton Orient. Seems you made quite an impression, young man.'

'Stop muckin' about, sir.'

'I'm serious. Offering you a trial.'

I stopped and stared at him, distracted slightly by the condensation in his salt-and-pepper moustache. 'You never said anything about scouts coming to the game.'

'That's 'cause I didn't know, boy. They don't announce it, you know, otherwise you lot get all nervous and can't perform.'

I tried hard not to smile. 'They want me to go for a trial?

'Yep.'

'Only me?'

'That's what your man said.'

'When?'

'Next Tuesday.'

'But that's a school day, sir.'

'Don't worry about that.'

With my excitement rising, I pictured myself making my professional debut for the O's, scoring the winner and celebrating in front of the home supporters. Mr. Ludlow brought me back to reality.

'Now listen, son, if I were you, I'd keep this thing under my hat for now. The other lads don't know yet. Best to wait and see how it goes before you...'

I didn't hear the rest. I sprinted to the dressing room to brag to my teammates. When I got there I was surprised to see that they'd arranged themselves into a guard-of-honour. Glen Barlow, team captain and Emlyn Hughes look-alike, started clapping and the other boys quickly joined in. Grinning, I walked slowly between them, my boots clack-clacking against the mud-spattered concrete floor. Along the way I got slapped about the head and kicked up the backside and at one point my strike partner, Deadly Darren Davis, said, 'Taught you everything you know.' I was about to deliver a comeback when Mr. Ludlow strode into the dressing room with a netful of balls slung over his shoulder.

'OK, OK, break it up there now. He's only going for a trial.'

'Yeah,' said Darren, 'for Orient.'

My teammates fell about laughing but I didn't care. Nothing was going to spoil my mood. A little while later, as I was peeling off my hot sweaty socks and struggling to breathe through the cloying smell of dubbing and Deep Heat, I started daydreaming again. In an extension of my earlier fantasy, the Orient fans were now chanting my name.

When I came home that day, I immediately asked my parents if I could go and play out. From our living room window on the second floor I could see Mitch and Benjy having a kick-about in the street and was desperate to go and tell them my news. My parents were in a good mood. That afternoon Mum had won a bit of money at bingo and she and Dad were enjoying a rare Saturday in together. I had got back from the match to find them cuddling on the plastic covered settee, listening to soul music and drinking cherry wine. But no matter their high spirits, I still couldn't go out before I'd had a bath and changed my clothes and put my dirty kit in the laundry basket. By the time I got outside, my earlier excitement had all but vanished.

Mitch and Benjy lived in the same street as me: two doors apart from each other and seven down from my house. I couldn't remember ever seeing one without the other. Mitch's parents were divorced. An only child, he lived with his mother Josette, a thin, wig-wearing, serious woman with permanently bloodshot eyes. She ran an all-night shebeen and was rarely seen during the day. We called her Countess Dracula. Mitch mostly had to fend for himself and hated his mother for it. Feeling sorry for him, my parents would regularly invite him in for dinner. Benjy's home life was equally troubled. His mother, Muriel, had mental problems and had once been committed. She never left the house. For as long as I'd known her, she'd been on one form of medication or another and was officially too sick to work. She had another child by another man, a girl two years older than Benjy called Cheryl, but had lost contact with her after the father won custody of the girl and moved to Birmingham. Benjy had never seen his half-sister and claimed that he never thought of her. His father, Charlie, sold weed from their house and was rumoured to be pimping out his mother, a rumour he, the father, fiercely denied and was prepared to fight over. Benjy was forever worried about his mother but he didn't know what he could do to help her. He found the atmosphere at home suffocating and, like Mitch, spent whatever free time he had playing football in our street, in all weathers.

'Serious?' said Benjy, spinning the ball on his forefinger. He was almost lost behind his black knee-length duffle coat.

'Why you lying?' said Mitch. He, too, was dressed against the cold in a red parka with a fur-line hood pulled over his head.

'I'm not!' I shrieked.

'Then swear on your mum's life,' said Mitch. He grabbed the ball from Benjy and started doing keep-ups.

I put my hand on my heart. 'I swear on my mum's life that Orient have asked me to come for a trial.'

Mitch squinted at me, searching my eyes. 'Nah,' he said, finally, 'don't believe you.' I felt like kicking him in the balls. He turned to Benjy, who was still doing keep-ups, and patted his chest. 'Put it here, Benj. If you can.'

Using his instep, Benjy deftly lobbed the ball towards Mitch who trapped it with his chest, let it roll onto his knee and then he too started doing keep-ups. They had skills, could perform all sorts of tricks with a ball, but they'd never been able to transfer that ability to a pitch. That's why they had never made their school team (they went to Upton House). They were what we called back then, 'street ballers', great for a kick-about but useless in a proper game.

'Just admit it,' said Mitch. 'You're telling porkies.'

I pushed him hard in the chest, sending him sprawling across the bonnet of our neighbour's yellow Cortina. He peeled himself off the car and was about to come at me when Mum threw open our living-room window and leaned out. 'No fighting!' Mitch was raging but didn't dare do anything with Mum watching. I gave him the finger and went inside.

I headed straight to my room, flung myself on my bed and lay there mentally abusing Mitch. After a few minutes I heard the theme tune from *Black Beauty*, through the plasterboard wall that separated my bedroom from the living room. For something to do, I got up and padded across the room to my cluttered study desk and sat there leafing through my latest copy of *Shoot! Magazine*. From the centre of it, I ripped a glossy double-page poster of Steve Perryman and selloptaped it to the wall above my desk. It was the latest in a growing collection of posters featuring Spurs players, past and present. My favourite, occupying pride of place in the centre of the wall, showed Glenn Hoddle wheeling away in celebration after scoring against Arsenal in the North London Derby.

I went to the trial by myself, by bus. Dad had wanted to take me but, as ever, his job came first. Before going off to work, Mum got up early and made me a packed lunch of corned beef sandwiches, but I was so nervous I knew I was never going to eat them. The trial was being held on a windy training pitch near the club's stadium in Leytonstone. I arrived an hour early, partly to create the right impression with the coaching staff, partly to give myself time to get a feel for the set up, but mostly because I was impatient to get going. I'd hardly slept the night before and was up and dressed before dawn. Unsure as to what the arrangements would be with regards to the changing facilities, I'd come kitted out and ready for action. What the other trialists were wearing I don't remember, but I had on my favourite Spurs replica shirt, the one with Glenn Hoddle's name stitched on the back. I had been looking forward to showing it off, so I was disappointed when, just before the trial began, we were issued with coloured bibs.

After much standing around, the trial finally got underway. Once we had run around the pitch a few times to warm up, the youth-team coach gathered us in the centre circle. He said we would be playing a straight eleven-a-side match, lasting an hour. He then gave us our positions – he put me up front – and told us to relax and play our natural game. 'Don't try too hard to impress, just enjoy it.' There we were on the threshold of realising the ambition of almost every schoolboy in the country. This was the biggest moment of our lives. Our futures hung in the balance. *Relax and play your natural game.* Fat chance. The pressure I felt to perform was almost crippling. During the match, I couldn't even get the basics right. My first touch went completely. I couldn't pass the ball two yards. My shooting lacked not only accuracy but power, as though my legs were made of straw. Because of my height, the midfield players kept lumping the ball up to me, in true English style, but I can't remember winning a single-header.

Basically, I had a stinker. At the end of the game, the coach was so embarrassed for me he couldn't look me in the eye. The fact that I'd scored quite a decent goal, an instinctive finish on the half-volley, made no difference. The coach told us that those who had been successful would be contacted, by letter, within a couple of weeks and that if we hadn't heard back by then, we should assume we wouldn't be.

Those two weeks felt like the longest of my life. Each morning I'd run downstairs to see if the postman had brought anything for me. While I was waiting for news I played again for my school team. In the changing room before the game Mr. Ludlow asked me how the trial had gone. 'I played shit.' My teammates started laughing. Deadly Darren said, 'So what's new?' I told him to go fuck himself and we almost came to blows. Mr. Ludlow had to step between us. Before we ran out to play, he took me to one side and did his best to put me back together. 'I'm sure you didn't do as bad as all that. You just never know with these people. Best to stay positive.'

A fortnight passed and still I hadn't heard anything. I waited another week, just to be sure, before accepting that I'd missed out. I was so downhearted I don't think I ever fully recovered. Outwardly I tried to give the impression that I hadn't been affected, that I had only suffered a flesh wound, when in truth the cut had been deep. I went through the motions, in case I was accused of giving up after the first setback. On Mr. Ludlow's advice I started attending open trials, concentrating on the lower leagues where I felt I had more chance of success; none of the clubs showed any interest. With each new rejection I sank further into myself, becoming so silent and withdrawn that my parents thought seriously about consulting a child psychologist, but their sympathy and understanding only went so far.

The day they received a letter from school to say that I'd only shown up for twelve lessons in the last month and that I'd be prevented from taken my exams if I didn't significantly improve my attendance record, they reverted to type. Dad, who always lapsed into patois when he became angry, called me 'wutless' and said I was destined to turn out like Theodore. Mum's forecast for my future was even more dire. Instead of Theodore, she used Mitch as an example of where I was headed. Mitch had now left home and set up in a squat and started signing on. Mum was trying to scare me but the picture she painted seemed very attractive. I was fifteen years old and felt it was time I got out from under my parents. Mitch had shown me a way. I ran into Benjy one day after school and we started talking excitedly about a time when the three of us would share a place, free from parental controls, where we could do what the hell we liked, when we liked. By the time we got home we had all but made the decision to move in with Mitch, but a few days later Benjy said he'd been having second thoughts. 'It's Mum. I can't leave her. She's getting worse, Si.' 'But can't your old man look after her?' He shook his head. 'You seen him lately?' 'Not in a while, no.' 'He's on smack.'

I moved in with Mitch. We didn't come to any formal arrangement. I started hanging out at his place and sort of stayed. For a week I didn't go home. I knew that Mum and Dad must have been sick with worry but I wanted to prove to myself that I could live independently of them. When my conscience became too heavy I went to see them. I made sure to call them first, to avoid any surprises and to give us all a chance to prepare, and it worked. Mum cried but she didn't get angry. Relieved to see that I looked well-fed, clean and that I wasn't going about in rags, she asked me how I'd been surviving for money. 'I'm signing on.' She shook her head, knowing full well what this meant. Dad, as I had expected, couldn't resist being condescending. 'You think you is a man? Well now you will learn what it is to live like one.' He then offered me money, I refused it and he smiled: 'You learn fast, I say that for you.'

Once the novelty had worn off, I realised that living in a squat wasn't quite what I had imagined. We didn't have to pay rent, but everything else about the experience was a pain. We had regular run-ins with Hackney Council, who used various bullying tactics to try to evict us. We once came home to find the place boarded up back and front. It took us almost the entire day to remove the boards, nail-by-nail, plank-by-plank, and re-occupy the house. They then served us an eviction notice and threatened legal action if we didn't vacate the property by the specified date. Mitch consulted the Citizens Advice Bureau and was told that we couldn't be evicted without being re-housed. We wrote back to the council to say that after taking legal advice, we were asserting our rights as squatters and would not be moving out unless we were offered a suitable alternative. After that their letters dried up. We thought we'd heard the last of them but then one morning an official came by, a young white guy with gelled ginger hair, claiming that he needed to inspect the place to make sure it was legally habitable. Stupidly we let him in, hoping to convince him that we were not running the place down, but almost as soon as he got in he started making notes and never spoke to us again except to ask directions to this room or that.

As was usually the case when visitors came calling, I saw nothing but defects in the property: the peeling masonry, the missing floorboards, the exposed circuitry. Mitch, suspicious as ever, followed the inspector around, standing over his shoulder while he scribbled into his notepad. Feeling worn out from a lack of sleep – we'd been out the night before – I went and sat on the collapsed settee. In front of me, on the milk crate-cum-coffee table was a bag of weed and some Rizlas and an ashtray overflowing with spliff roaches. It suddenly occurred to me that the inspector must have seen it all and that he had probably noticed the smell too. I quickly gathered up the evidence and hid them away. Moments later I heard Mitch's voice coming from the bathroom. He sounded angry so I went to investigate. When I got there I saw that he had the inspector by the throat.

'Get my blade, Si. I'm gonna mark my man for his fuckry talk.'

I panicked. The inspector's eyes were bloodshot and bulging. He was struggling to get free but though he was a grown man, and Mitch only a sixteen-year-old boy, he couldn't get away.

'What the fuck, Mitch!' I screamed. 'What's happened?'

'This guy's gotta be taught a lesson,' he growled, 'he can't chat to people like that. Who the fuck does he think he his?'

The inspector, his back against the wall, was going blue in the face and seemed on the brink of passing out.

'What did he say?' I asked. Mitch nodded towards the

96

toilet bowl. I looked in it and saw a couple of fat turds. I couldn't understand it. I had used the toilet only that morning and had flushed it and I knew that Mitch hadn't used it since.

'It's blocked,' I said.

'Yeah,' said Mitch. He tightened his grip on the inspector's throat. 'That's what I told hombre here. Told him we'd get it sorted as soon as. But the racist cunt says,' and here he mimicked the inspector's voice, '"I don't know how you people can live like this. You're no better than animals."' He kissed his teeth and added, 'What you waiting for, Si? Go get my tings, bredren. My man has to get two juk today.'

I couldn't believe what I was hearing. 'Mitch, let the guy go. What the fuck you doing? Think, man. Use your head. You can't just go round stabbing people for no reason.'

He gave me a look of disgust, as if he was about to spit in my face, then turned back to the inspector. Jabbing his finger in the man's face, he said, 'You're one lucky bredda, you know that?' He dropped his hand and the inspector collapsed to the ground, coughing and spluttering and gasping for air. Mitch was about to kick him but I stepped in.

'Just get the fuck out of here, Mitch. You're a nutter, I swear.'

'Fuck you too,' he barked, then stormed out.

I tried to help the inspector up but he shoved me away and swore that he was going straight to the police. I advised him not to do that, strongly, saying that Mitch would come after him, no matter how long it took and whatever the consequences and I meant it. If he was scared, the inspector didn't show it. He eventually got to his feet, told me to go 'stuff' myself and, holding his throat, staggered out. We never saw him or any other council official again and we heard nothing from the police. It seemed that we, or rather Mitch, had scared them off. But that wasn't the end of our troubles. We couldn't relax. Too many people had it in for us.

The two-storey, three-bedroom house was on a fairly smart, residential street near Victoria Park, tree-lined and quiet. Our neighbours included GPs and estate agents. They saw us as little more than scum and would make their feelings known by scrawling graffiti on our front door: *Squatters Out!* Once they even got up a petition. It was signed by virtually every household in the street and delivered to the council. When that didn't work, they formed themselves into a residents group and started giving interviews to the *Hackney Gazette*, claiming that they didn't necessarily object to us squatting, only to the drugs and the loud music and the coming and going at all hours and to the way we had allowed the house to fall into disrepair. For almost a year, they kept at us. I wouldn't say they wore us down, but we decided to do something to get them off our backs.

We gathered up a work gang, including Benjy, who'd been hanging out at the house so much he was as good as living there, and spent about two weeks painting the place, inside and out. It made a noticeable difference to the appearance of the property and to how we felt about living in it. We also tried, as best as teenagers can, to tone down the noise, especially at night, and out of respect to the young children in the street, we never smoked weed or drank alcohol in their presence. The neighbours didn't thank us, and we didn't expect them to, but gradually they came to accept us. We weren't going anywhere, so unless they moved, and given that the law was on our side, they had little choice. After that, the only issue we had was with the electricity suppliers. Aware that we were squatting, they insisted on installing a meter, which meant many an interrupted TV programme and some very gloomy candle-lit nights.

I should have been happy. I had left home, was living an independent life, but the truth was my self-esteem had never been lower. Surviving on the dole robbed me of my pride, my self-respect. Mitch didn't see it that way. 'Black people have suffered plenty at the hands of the white man. They owe us.' That was one way of looking at it but it was not a view I shared. Every time I went to sign on I felt worthless, a scrounger, a leech. I started looking for work. Without any qualifications I struggled, but eventually I landed a job working at Wimpy in Piccadilly Circus. The manager, Neil, a fitness fanatic with muscles in his face, made life very difficult for the black workers, all teenagers like myself. He would put us on the worst jobs – cleaning the toilets, emptying the rubbish, clearing and wiping down the tables, mopping the floor – whilst reserving the cashier duties for himself and the other white staff. A strict timekeeper, he would tap his watch if you showed up even a minute late for your shift and he expected you to make up the time before you left. Career advancement opportunities were non-existent. It would have taken me years just to become a supervisor, without any additional pay, and to become a manager meant being white and connected to the people who made the promotions. Speaking of pay, I was working an average of fifty hours a week with over-time and barely getting by. When I factored in the cost of commuting from Hackney to the west end, I worked out that I was actually better off on the dole. And so, after six months, I quit and went back to signing on.

While I'd been getting up early every morning and going to work, Mitch had been out thieving and had turned the squat into an Aladdin's Cave of stolen goods. Benjy had dropped out of school, too. He still hadn't officially moved in but he slept over most nights, only going home occasionally to see how his mum was getting on and to bring her some money. His dad had gone from chasing the dragon to mainlining and was now in no fit state to take care of himself, let alone his wife.

Because it contained so many valuables, we had to protect the squat against break-ins. The back and front doors were grilled and padlocked and there were burglar-bars on all the lower-floor windows. As well as securing our things, this level of protection proofed us against police raids and made dealing much easier, something Benjy had started doing in imitation of his father. We had always smoked weed, even at school, so it made sense to now be selling the stuff. But we couldn't really get going on it. Our customers came by in dribs and drabs, their numbers were not sufficient for us to make any real money. We were too out of the way in Victoria Park. We needed to be closer to the action, we needed to be on the Frontline.

* * *

Sandringham Road – aka the Frontline or the Front – had a reputation to rival Railton Road in Brixton and All Saints Road in Ladbroke Grove. With its West Indian takeaway shops and makeshift poolrooms, dingy basement shebeens and dilapidated dope dens, it attracted people from all sections of Hackney's black community and beyond. We first went there to buy weed wholesale, from a contact Benjy had made through his father, but once we saw the level of street trade that was going on, we set up shop. It was a man's world, which is to say there were very few women, but it was cross-generational. Teenagers rubbed shoulders with men in their forties and fifties, with us youngsters cast in the role of 'cadets'. We regulars came to be known as the Sandringham Massive, and I take no pride in saying that our in-your-face, couldn't-give-a-shit, fuck-you attitude won us few friends in the wider community. This was especially true of the police. To them we were not only a bunch of criminals but also the enemy. We had no love for them either. To provoke us, they would post sentries at either end of the Front and all the roads leading off it, making it easier for them to spot who was coming and going and to carry out 'stop and search'. They had us under siege. Occasionally we'd rise to the bait and lob a few bricks and bottles at them, and maybe the odd Molotov cocktail, but they were always careful not to engage us in running battles. This was 1983, two years after the Brixton Riots. They were scared.

Selling weed on the Frontline was not, and had never been, my idea of a life. As time passed I began to lose interest in it and started casting around for something to do that would free me from what I had now come to see as a kind of prison. I was growing up, mentally and physically, I was becoming a man, but what did that mean exactly? I thought a lot about what my father had said. 'You think you is a man? Well you will now learn what it is to live like one.'

There were some contradictions I needed to figure out. My parents worked hard, too hard in my opinion, yet they could only dream about taking a holiday or buying a car or even eating out now and then. They longed to own their own home. For as long as I could remember they'd been putting money aside for a down payment on a mortgage, but as quickly as it went into their savings account it came back out again to pay off hire-purchase debts or to help some relative or another in Jamaica. The begging letters arrived almost by the week.

They were still relatively young, my parents, barely into their forties, but already the pressure of keeping their lives afloat had given Dad grey hairs and Mum psoriasis, well-known as a stress-related skin condition. I might not have wanted to become a career weed dealer, but I didn't want my parents' life either. The gap between these two alternatives seemed so wide as to be unbridgeable. I felt confused. I simply didn't know what to do with myself. I started eavesdropping on the conversations of those handful of Rastas who always seemed to be knocking about on the Front. I say conversations but they actually called it 'reasoning'. One guy in particular, Ras Malachi, a Jamaican who'd been in the country since the early seventies and whose grey-flecked dreads went down to his calves, became almost like a spiritual guide to me. His mantra was 'Peace and Love', but no one mistook him for being passive. He would defend himself against all forms of attack, mental or physical, and was especially aggressive when it came to protecting the reputation and legacy of Haile Selassie.

I'll always remember the day he and Django clashed. Django, a recently-arrived Yardie who was generally accepted as the baddest man on the Front, started goading the Ras by suggesting that his faith was demeaned for having Selassie as its godhead. But just as no Christian would ever accept that Christ wasn't the Messiah, and just as no Muslim would ever dream of denying Mohammed his status as the Prophet, so no true Rasta would seriously entertain the heretical notion of Haile Selassie being anything other than God incarnate, or a Prophet, or, as Ras Malachi called him that day, 'The King of Kings, the Lord of Lords, the Conquering Lion of the tribe of Judah.'

He was leaning against a piece of corrugated iron covered with posters featuring some of the biggest reggae artists of the day – Dennis Brown, Gregory Isaacs, Black Uhuru – and the backdrop seemed to add weight and authority to his arguments. When Django tried to challenge him, saying that Selassie had been given his titles falsely, Ras Malachi laughed, fingered his beard which tapered down to his chest like a wizard's, and said, 'You don't know your scripture, me I-dren.'

Django became more and more animated, even confrontational. While he spoke, he kept his ratchet knife in his hand the whole time. His finger was looped in the ring and he kept spinning and catching it, spinning and catching it, like a gunslinger. He was wearing a red beret perched on one side of his mini-afro, a black silk shirt, drain-pipe trousers with the legs turned up to show off his diamond-patterned socks and Clarks desert boots with the laces removed. Like all the other Yardies, he thought he had a great dress sense, but he just looked gaudy. Eventually he and Malachi drew quite an audience. Malachi had his sympathisers. A few of his Rasta friends were standing nearby and to almost everything he said, they added, often in unison, 'Rastafari'. Django had his own supporters, Yardies all, about ten of them in total, including a few women. The rest of the crowd were supposed to be neutral, but were obviously rooting for Malachi. I know I was. Django was all noise and posturing, playing to his people, whereas Malachi spoke with a calm authority. I could have listened to him all day. The man was not only a natural orator, he had charisma to spare, and much of that was down to the way he looked.

On that day, his locks were piled high on his head in coils, the weight forcing him to keep his neck straight to avoid drooping. It had made him aware of his posture, which was regally erect. A strict vegetarian, non-alcoholic diet and had given his body a trim, youthful look that belied his fifty-odd years. He was wearing a pair of ironed khaki trousers and a short-sleeve khaki shirt with the collar buttoned up, the outfit enhanced by a beaded necklace and a wooden pendant carved in the shape of Africa. He seemed to ooze knowledge and wisdom. I was drawn to him, began to see him almost as a substitute father. If there was chance to pick his brain, I jumped on it. He knew a thirsty person when he saw one and did what he could to slake my thirst. Over time we became very close, in a teacher-pupil sort of way. It was almost inevitable that he'd end up trying to convert me.

I didn't become a Rasta, not in the strictest sense, but I was a 'fashion dread' for a while, meaning that although I had the dreadlocks and smoked the chalice, although I accompanied Ras Malachi to Jah Shaka's dances and wore the weatherman tam and the red, yellow and green clothing, although I knew a little something about Nyabinghi and could quote a few passages of scripture, I just couldn't bring myself to 'bow' to Selassie or give up pork or accept Ethiopia as my spiritual home and the birthplace of mankind or look upon Bob Marley and Marcus Garvey as holy prophets. It's not nice to be called a false anything, but, to borrow from Marley, the cap fitted me and so I wore it. Ras Malachi was sympathetic. 'Following Jah is not a easy road. Babylon make it hard for the youth. Like you, many of them get the call but only a few answer.' He was certainly right about that. I wasn't the only 'fashion dread' in the neighbourhood. There were plenty of my peers who knew the recipe for Rastafarianism but couldn't cook the meal. Like me, they would pepper their speech with Rasta-isms – *Jah know, Jah bless, Rastafari, Selassie I, Ital, Irie, Bal'head, Livity, Babylon* – without any real understanding of what they were saying.

Even so, some of the things I learned from Ras Malachi have stayed with me ever since. For instance, it was he who encouraged me to question the accepted version of who Jesus was. Christ, he said, was not born of a virgin, and was most certainly not a blue-eyed, blond-haired Caucasian, but in fact a black man, or at the very least a man of dark complexion. It's hard for me to describe the feeling I had when I first heard this said. The image of a white Christ was so embedded in my consciousness that it felt almost blasphemous for me to try to think of him in any other way. I realised that I'd been so conditioned into regarding anything black as negative that I couldn't picture Christ as a black man without experiencing a pang of fear, as though I expected to be struck by lightning. This reluctance to question accepted truths, particularly those which, deliberately or not, directly or otherwise, put black people in a position of inferiority, was something I had to work hard to eradicate from my subconscious, and there's a good chance that had I not been exposed to Rastafari, had I not met Ras Malachi, I might never have begun the process.

* * *

I met Beverly on the Front. She used to buy weed from us. Tall, thin and athletic, with close-cropped hair that she often dyed blonde and with a boho dress sense that made her look like the popstar she had once dreamed of becoming, I fancied her as soon as I saw her. Pregnant at fourteen, while still at school, she lived on benefits in a high-rise council flat on the Berry Street Estate. When I met her she was sixteen and had just split with her daughter's father, Rickie, who, unable to handle the responsibility of being a dad, had bolted. The whole experience – getting pregnant and giving birth, dropping out of school, moving out of her parents' place, being abandoned by her boyfriend when she needed him most – had left her bewildered. A lot of her child benefit went on weed, which she used as a kind of self-medication. Aside from playing with her daughter, nothing gave her more pleasure. She slept a lot and cried even more, silently, often while we were having sex, which she liked to do in the dark. I guess she was depressed, but at the time I was ignorant of such things and thought she was being self-indulgent.

Other teenage mothers I knew were getting on with it, making plans for the future, taking evening classes, working part-time and drawing on the support of their relatives to babysit so they could get out and now and then and let their hair down. Not Beverly. She was proud and stubborn, Miss Independent. After what had happened to her, she was reluctant to ask for help, least of all from her parents, who, she claimed, had unmasked themselves during her pregnancy. 'They couldn't wait to get me out the house. As soon as I told them I was pregnant they made me register for a council flat.'

I once made the mistake of suggesting that she try to make things up with Rickie so he could become more of a regular feature in his daughter's life. 'You must be joking. He can go to hell. Him and his bitch sisters.'

The reference to the sisters was telling. It turned out that Rickie had been thinking of making a go of things but had been persuaded from doing so by his two sisters. They had never liked Beverly and believed she had deliberately gotten herself pregnant (she was supposed to have been on the pill) to trap their brother. They went to her house and accused her of it. 'I told those two slags where to get off. And I told Rickie that he should think for himself and that if he couldn't, I didn't want him in my life.' That ended things between them. It was, she said, the excuse Rickie had been waiting for. Now, their only contact was when they ran into each other in the street.

I dreaded being out and about with Beverly when that happened. The situation was just too awkward. Beverly never had much to say to Rickie and so he was forced to talk to his daughter. Picking her up, you could almost predict what he was going to say. 'Who's my little girl, eh? God, you're getting so big. You being a good girl for mummy? Give daddy a kiss.' On one occasion I said to Beverly, 'I'll catch you later babes, give you guys a bit of time alone,' and she said, 'What you on about? I don't need no time alone with him.' I didn't know where to put my face. Neither did Rickie.

We'd been seeing each other for about six months when Beverly asked me to move in. I'd been spending more time at her place than the squat, which had become too much of a 'spot' to have any kind of privacy, so it made sense. Mitch thought I was crazy, or, as he called it, 'pussy whupped'. He saw the situation for what it was: I was a sixteen-year-old boy who was giving up his hard-earned freedom for a ready-made-family and bills. Benjy didn't feel strongly about it one-way or the other, but he wondered whether I wasn't allowing myself to be exploited. 'Don't let my girl bleed you dry. That's all I'll say.' I wasn't worried about that. Beverly had never asked me for money, not for herself, not for her daughter. I contributed to the rent, gas and electricity bills but never felt under any pressure to do so. The truth is we got on really well.

I couldn't keep pace with the speed of the changes happening in my life. I missed my brother. He was the one person I'd had always been able to talk to, but now I could never pin him down as he was hardly ever around, he was too busy running around London robbing people. He had always been into petty crime, but after he left home he got into some really heavy stuff, the sort of thing we had grown up watching on programmes like *The Sweeney*, the kind involving balaclavas and saw-off shotguns.

I don't know how or where he met them, but at some point he got involved with a serious set of white guys – proper villains who could trace their criminal roots back to the Krays – and became an armed robber. For about three years, between the ages of eighteen and twenty-one, he and his gang went on a crime spree that made his name ring out in the neighbourhood. And how he lived up to his image. He wore nothing but designer suits and animal skin shoes, ostrich being his particular favourite. On the rare occasions that I saw him, he would take me on shopping sprees to the west end and buy me the most expensive outfits. On the way back, he would make sure to cruise along the Front so everyone could see all the designer shopping bags we had stuffed in the back seat of his Bimmer. I got a lot of respect just from being his brother. My only regret during this period was that I didn't see enough of him, a few times a year if I was lucky. He'd go missing for months at a stretch, usually after he'd pulled one of his jobs, and then, out of nowhere, he'd show up, looking sharp and dripping in jewellery. He'd never hang around for more than a day or two and, constantly worried about being grassed up, could never stay in one place for more than a few hours at a time. He was a Londoner through and through, but he seemed to spend most of his time hiding out with his gang on the continent. I believe I still have a few of the postcards he sent me from places like the Algarve and the Costa del Sol. Even now I don't think he appreciates just how much I looked up to him and just how saddened I was by his swift, surprising and spectacular fall.

By the mid-eighties, almost without warning, crack cocaine had arrived in our midst. It felt as though I'd gone to bed one night and woken up the next morning to find the world had changed beyond all recognition. Recreational drugs like weed and hash had become old hat. Everyone was now either sniffing Charlie or freebasing it. Cocaine had become the trendiest drug in town. The demand for it was such that it quickly became readily available and cheap.

In the media there were endless doomsday predictions about Britain's inner cities going the way of America's, that is to say awash with crack addicts who would turn to crime to support their habits. The prediction proved to be accurate, but not to the extent that some had forecast. Britain's inner cities were not destroyed by crack in the same way that America's had been. But it didn't matter, for in as much as it galvanised the police and the courts, the scaremongering did its damage. I knew people who served long stretches in prison for being caught in possession of a few crack rocks, and not all of them were dealers. I used cocaine occasionally, as did Mitch and Benjy, but whilst there was a fair amount of money to be made from selling it, we didn't have the stomach for what was a vicious, cut-throat, kill-or-be-killed business. We were weed sellers and stuck to that.

Theodore, on the other hand, had no such qualms. As well as his regular work holding up building societies, he had diversified into selling cocaine. At first he restricted himself to dealing wholesale, driving around in his car with kilos of the stuff in his boot, but then he made the classic mistake of getting high on his own supply. Soon he could be seen hustling rocks on the Front like any common street dealer. His habit sky-rocketed as rapidly as his reputation plummeted. In less than a year, he became a wreck. It made me deeply ashamed to see him shuffling around the neighbourhood, looking dirty and unshaven, begging, borrowing and stealing in an increasingly desperate attempt to maintain his habit.

Daily, he would pester me for money to buy drugs; over time I lost all respect for him and began cursing him openly in the streets. I would use the most foul and abusive language in the hope that he might be humiliated into getting his act together. I was wasting my breath. I lost sleep worrying about him, as did my parents, who, to my surprise, had taken him in when he had nowhere to live. He and they were constantly arguing, mostly about the fact that he was stealing money from them and slowly selling off their possessions. Eventually they lost patience with him and, for the second time in his life, threw him out.

It was then that he moved in with me and Beverly. The place was barely big enough for one person, never mind four. Beverly was not happy at all when I asked her if my brother could stay with us for a while, and when she discovered he was on crack, she flatly refused to put him up. I had to beg her, and even then she only relented on the strict agreement that Theodore never smoked crack in the flat and that he'd be gone after a month at the longest. Not only did he smoke crack in the house, he stayed with us for over six months. In that time we became almost like parents to him. We had to make sure he ate, washed and slept a little now and then. We had to buy him clothes, which he would wear until they were literally stiff with dirt and grime. Very occasionally, he'd have a lucid moment and the horrible reality of what he'd become would dawn on him. Often with tears in his eyes, he would talk to me about his desire to get clean and, as he put it, 'get back in the game'. But nothing ever changed. Lacking the will to get better, he couldn't find the way. His nightmare continued, month after depressing month. And then, out of the blue, everything came to a head. One night, long after I'd left the Front and gone back to Beverly's, Benjy came round to our place with the news that Theodore had been repeatedly stabbed by Django for trying to exchange a fake gold chain for a couple of crack rocks.

When I went to see him in hospital Theodore could neither open his eyes nor speak. I started crying. For something to do, I picked up his limp hand and held it in mine. He had been given a massive blood transfusion but still looked close to death. The doctors expected him to make a slow but full recovery. Looking at him, it didn't seem possible. Mum and Dad showed up a while later. For several minutes they did nothing but stand and stare, as if they couldn't quite believe their eyes. Mitch and Benjy had come with me to the hospital and were hovering in the background, trying to be discreet. I remember that Benjy kept shaking his head and that Mitch was grinding his teeth so hard his jawline was rippling. None of us spoke.

No-one said anything. They didn't need to. I knew what was expected of me and was deeply afraid, both of what I had to do and the person I'd be going up against. Django was a killer. By all accounts, most of them his own, he'd been killing since he was in short pants. I'd heard him bragging about the amount of people he'd murdered, often for the most trifling reason. I'd listened, open-mouthed, while he and his boys gave gloating details of all the people they had gunned down in the slums of Kingston, laughing and joking about how their victims had begged for their lives before being shot, usually in

112

the face. His reputation alone made it difficult even to look at him. Most people on the Front, including some of his own gang, were terrified of him.

Even assuming I had the courage to take him on, which I didn't, how was I going to do it? I'd seen my fair share of violence, had grown up around it, it was nothing new to me, yet apart from the odd fight at school, I'd never personally been involved in anything serious. Mitch often used to talk about stabbing people's guts out, laughing about how he would leave their innards in their lap like a bowl of spaghetti. Just thinking about the image was enough to make me nauseous. And yet I carried a knife, we all did, more as a deterrent than anything. If people knew you were armed they'd think twice, or so the theory went. In any case I felt fortunate that so far I'd never been tested, never been backed into a corner to the point where I felt I had to use a knife on someone. As for guns, I didn't know the first thing about them. I'd never seen one in my life, much less handled or fired any. I wouldn't have known where to start if I wanted to get hold of one.

Despite all the gangster films I had watched, it was only after my brother had been stabbed that I properly understood the attraction of putting a contract on someone's head. You could have your way without getting your hands wet, so to speak. But I knew no-one in that line of work and even if I did, how would I pay them? And suppose for argument's sake say I managed to find someone and was able to pay, could I then live with myself knowing that I had financed the killing of another human being, even one as vile as Django? You don't go from being a choirboy to a killer in two years, unless you're a psychopath. I knew which side of the divide I lived on I was keen to remain there. There was, I believed, such a thing as wickedness.

What I wanted to do to Django was wicked and yet, if I stopped to think about what he had done to Theodore, if I pictured my brother on his drip, if I ever stopped and thought about how close he had come to dying and how he must have suffered while he was being stabbed over and over, if I dwelt on the fact that he'd been left bleeding on the street, I could actually feel the evil rising in my body. I hated Django. Deep down inside I throbbed with the desire to get even with him but to do that I'd have to become another person. Someone like Mitch. He had violence in him. It was only a matter of time before he gave full vent to it. I pitied the person who eventually fell victim to his rage and I pitied him for having to contend with it night and day. Benjy, who had once taken a kitchen knife to his own father for slapping his mother, was like a tree-hugger in comparison. They wanted to help me. They'd known me all my life and knew I didn't have it in me to take Django down, not by myself anyhow.

On the night of the stabbing, on the bus ride back from the hospital, Mitch said, 'You ain't alone in this, Si. Man's got your back.' 'For real,' said Benjy. I nodded but didn't say anything. I didn't know what to say. I didn't know how to tell them I was scared and that I was secretly hoping the police would get me out of my bind. They had begun an investigation into the attack, had actually shown up on the Front and asked questions, but no one dared go on the record against Django, and since Theodore was still unable to speak and was not going to identify his attacker when he recovered, the investigation was unlikely to go anywhere.

The day after the attack I stayed at home. I didn't go to the Front because I was too scared but I heard that Django had showed up there as normal. He didn't fear me in the slightest. He was taunting me. There was no other way for me to look at it. Beverly advised me to let the matter drop but even she knew what it would mean for me if I didn't act. One evening Mitch stopped by to check whether I was going to do something or, as he put it, 'pussy out'. I got annoyed. 'For fuck's sake! It's my brother. Let me deal with this in my way.' I'd raised my voice, which got Beverly's hackles up. 'Keep it down, please. If you wanna argue, take it outside. Shereen's asleep.' Mitch left, calling me a coward under his breath. I was glad to see the back of him. At that moment, he seemed to represent everything that was wrong in my life.

For the next couple of days I hid myself away at home, getting under Beverly's feet, smoking weed and worrying about the damage I was doing to my reputation by staying away from the Front. The only thing that drew me from the house was Theodore. He was still in hospital but was now sitting up and talking a little. On one visit, after he'd heard me spouting my empty threats, he lost patience and said, 'I wish you'd stop chatting shit. It ain't you, bruv. Never was. You trying to end up in here with me? Please, do me a favour and stop going on about it.' I was moved by his concern for my safety, but questioning my courage was extremely hard to take. It hurt me and made me determined to prove him wrong. Even here, with so much at stake, my lifelong desire to please him, to gain his approval, seemed to be overriding all other considerations. It occurred to me that he might have been biding his time till he was well again before taking his own revenge on Django. He was no coward, so it seemed logical. In all likelihood, he was plotting something, but I couldn't allow him to get the job done ahead of me. It was mine to do. He knew it. I knew it. Everyone knew it.

* * *

The first time I met Lee he made me jump. I'd just come back from the hospital and was about to take the lift up to the twelfth floor, covering my nose against the stench coming from the nearby rubbish chute, when he stepped in front of me and said. 'Name's Lee. Friend of your brother's. Got a minute?' I looked him up and down: white, clean-shaven, twenty-something, about five-ten, dressed in a blue overcoat, black drainpipe trousers and brown suede loafers. I'd never met any of Theodore's old gang before and hadn't expected any of them to look so dapper. Now I understood why he always used to dress so well, it had obviously been part of their identity. For a moment I wondered if they had given themselves a gang name, something sartorial. The Burberry Boys, for example. I had a quick look around, suddenly wondering if he was alone. There was no one else about. It had just gone nine and the flats were always quiet at that time of night.

Turning back to Lee I said, 'I'm listening.'

'Bit public, don't you think?' He pulled a face and added, 'Not to mention whiffy.'

'What's this about?'

'Your brother.'

'What about him?'

'We heard what happened.'

A door opened on the first floor balcony, directly above our heads. We couldn't see the person and instinctively stopped talking and listened as he or she shuffled along the landing and put something in the rubbish chute. Moments later it landed with a loud thud in the metal bin a few feet from where we stood. After the person had gone back inside and closed the door Lee said, 'There's a boozer not two minutes from here. Fancy a swift one? On me?'

We ended up in a faded pub in Haggerston. It was deserted except for a few old white guys who were sitting at a round table nursing pints, smoking cigarettes and chatting in hushed tones. The table was so small their knees were practically touching. Lee was much more comfortable in that environment than I was. As soon as we walked in his shoulders went back, his chest seemed to expand and he became altogether more confident than when he had approached me in the flats. I hung back as he strode up to the counter and ordered a pint of lager for himself and a Jack Daniels and Coke for me. The barman, a paunchy white guy with bad teeth and a comb-over, looked at me and said to Lee, 'Is he old enough to drink?' I laughed. I'd never been ID'd before. Lee said, 'It's OK,' and the barman silently prepared our drinks. I took the opportunity to look around. I couldn't remember the last time I'd been in a pub. They were places to be avoided. Racist white people went to pubs. That was the first deterrent. The second was that they always had musty old carpets and reeked of cigarette smoke, stale alcohol and sweat. This one was no different, on the décor and smell at least.

We took our drinks over to a secluded corner near the dartboard and sat face to face across a rectangular table with four Watneys beer mats and a dirty metal ashtray on it. The lighting in that part of the pub was dim but not so much that you couldn't see the rings on the table and the crumbs on the brown Paisley carpet. We clinked glasses and Lee said, 'To Theodore. Here's hoping he makes a speedy recovery.'

He took a sip of his lager, which left him with a thin line of froth on his top lip, then put his glass down and said, 'T's a top bloke. Honestly, he's like a brother to us. We couldn't believe it when we heard.'

He paused, fingered the rim of his glass, then added, 'Do you know who did it?'

'Don't you?'

'Wouldn't be asking if I did.'

'I know who it was. And believe me, he ain't getting away with it.'

'Oh yeah?'

'Yeah.' I sipped my drink for the first time, the ice already beginning to melt. It was a little too light on the whisky and way too heavy on the Coke.

'Anything we can do to help?'

I became suspicious. It suddenly occurred to me that I'd never met this guy before. For all I knew he was Old Bill.

'How do you know my brother again?'

Lee smiled and said, 'Smart boy.'

He then told me a story from my early childhood, involving a bed-wetting incident that only Theodore and my parents knew about. It made me laugh, both the story and the fact that Theodore had seen fit to tell his gang about it.

'Can you get me a gun?' It just came out.

Lee took a moment to recover from the surprise then said, 'Ever used one?'

'No.'

'There's all kinds of guns.' I didn't say anything, feeling slightly silly for being so non-specific.

Lee said, 'Something small but powerful, something you can conceal and carry around without too much trouble. That sound like the kind of thing you need?'

I sipped my drink. All of a sudden my throat felt parched and my heart was beating a bit too rapidly. I was only having a conversation but already I could feel myself crossing that divide. Lee must have sensed my fear because he said, 'You sure you wanna go down this road?'

I looked at him, taking a moment to consider the implications of what he was saying, then nodded.

'Alright, then. Leave it with me.'

He put his glass to his mouth, tilted his head back and downed the rest of his pint in one go, his Adam's apple bobbing and down as he swallowed. I waited for him to drain the glass then said,

'How much will it cost me?'

He looked surprised. 'You having a giggle? It's on the house.' He stood up and said, 'Fancy another?'

The following day he met me outside Dagenham Heathway station in his blue Triumph Stag. I felt grumpy, like someone being forced to do something he didn't want to do. As we were driving away from the station, Lee tried to engage me in conversation and it was all I could do not to tell him to shut up. Not only was he being too chirpy, his yellow Fila tracksuit, zipped up to his neck, was a little too loud and his aftershave a little too pungent. I couldn't wait to get away from him and

119

wondered how my brother had been able to spend so much time around guys like him. How he had even met them was still a mystery to me. He had always refused to discuss it with me, saying the less I knew about them the better it was for me. In the pub the night before, I had tried to get some answers from Lee but he'd been just as tight-lipped.

'T's right. Best not to ask a lot of questions.'

He did answer a couple, though. Had he or any of his gang been to see Theodore in hospital? 'No. Two of the lads are being detained at her Majesty's pleasure and the rest of us are on our toes.'

How did he hear about Theodore being stabbed?

'It was in the *Hackney Gazette*. Did you not see it?'

I hadn't.

We drove deeper into the countryside. Lee talked the whole way, mostly about all the rain we'd been having recently. He was all for it.

'Nothing better for staying indoors with the missus and getting all cosy, eh?'

I muttered a few words here and there, but my mind was on the business at hand. I kept my head turned away, staring at the passing scenery while Lee prattled on. After a while I saw that the clouds had started to darken, casting a gloomy shadow over the winding country lane and the hedges, trees and fields round and about.

The stables were in the middle of nowhere, surrounded on all sides by the Essex countryside. I counted twelve adjoining stalls, each with its own door. Aptly, they were laid out in the shape of a horseshoe, around a cobbled courtyard. The place was obviously well-kept. But for a few dead leaves blown in by the autumn winds, the yard looked immaculate. All the stalls were closed except two, which had their top flaps open. As we pulled into the yard, and no doubt attracted to the noise, a chestnut-coloured horse with a long, black, shiny mane poked its neck out from one of the open stalls.

When we got out of the car, it became excited and started moving its head up and down and flaring its nostrils as if in greeting. Lee hurried towards it. I stood back, not sure if I was supposed to follow, and watched as Lee started stroking the animal's neck and smoothing its ears and saying something to it which I didn't quite catch. After a while he noticed I hadn't moved and beckoned me over. Reluctantly – I was no animal lover – I walked across the courtyard. Once I was standing next to him, and at what I thought was a safe enough distance from the horse, Lee said, 'Simon, I'd like you to meet Fancy. Fancy, Simon.'

He then invited me to stroke the horse but I refused. It looked too big, too powerful. 'They bite don't they?'

'Only if provoked. Go on, she's friendly.'

Tentatively, I moved towards Fancy and slowly stretched out my hand towards her. She could tell I was nervous and seemed to want to help me. Lowering her head, she suddenly lunged forward and nudged my hand with her hot moist nose. The shock, to say nothing of the force, made me take a step back but Lee urged me forward again and this time I put my hand on her neck and left it there. She didn't move. Her neck muscles were big and taught, her skin velvet smooth and cool to the touch. Feeling more confident, I started moving my hand up and down her neck, along her mane and then finally over her ears and in the space between her eyes. A sense of peace and well-being came over me and the more I stroked the calmer I felt. Lee broke the spell by saying, 'She's a beauty isn't she?' I'd never been that close to a horse before, and had certainly never touched one.

I didn't know what else to say apart from, 'She's quite something.'

On the way from the station Lee had talked a bit about the stables and now went a little further into its history. It had been in his family for generations. They rented it out but business had become so slow they were thinking of converting the building into a luxury home and selling it off. Fancy actually belonged to his sister, Jean, who came out from Ilford on a daily basis to muck out her stall and take her for a gallop. While Lee was speaking, we were joined by a middle-aged man dressed in green mud-spattered wellies and a grey quilted body-warmer. He was accompanied by a black-and-white sheep dog who slinked away from me but started wagging its tail when it saw Lee. The man seemed to appear from nowhere but had actually driven into the courtyard in his mud-covered Land Rover. Lee introduced us. He was called Jim and his dog was called Lottie. Lee said I was a friend from London and I got the feeling Jim had heard that many times before. He grabbed my hand and shook it vigorously and said,

'I see you've met Fancy. Play your cards right and Lee here might let you ride her later.' Suddenly nervous again, I said, 'I don't know about that.'

They laughed, by which point Lottie had decided I was OK and started licking my trainers.

After a few more pleasantries, Jim went back to his Land Rover, opened the back and took out what looked like a small bingo bag, Lottie prancing about his legs the whole time and whining slightly. He came back and handed the bag to Lee and said, 'I forgot to ask: how's Shelley?' Lee brightened. 'She's fine, thanks. All over now.'

'Nice,' said Jim. 'Frank must be chuffed to bits.'

Lee nodded and said, 'So chuffed he's booked a cruise for the two of them. A fortnight around the Mediterranean.'

Jim smiled. 'Alright for some, eh?'

I tried to fill in the gaps. Lee was obviously talking about his parents. His mum had been ill and it must have been serious enough for his father to be taking her on a cruise to celebrate her recovery.

While I speculated, I couldn't take my eyes off the bag in Lee's hand. I knew what was in it and the thought made my heart pound, whereas Lee and Jim were chatting away like a couple of golf buddies taking a break between rounds.

'Well, Lottie,' said Jim, 'back to work for us. Let's leave these two idlers alone.'

We shook hands and he said, 'Nice to meet you, Simon. Good luck.'

Good luck? Did he know what I was planning to do? If he did, it hardly seemed appropriate that he should be wishing me good luck. I wasn't going on a pheasant hunt. He turned to Lee, 'As for you young man, I suppose I'll see you when I see you.'

'Not if I see you first.'

Jim rolled his eyes. 'The oldies are the best.'

'And you'd know all about that, wouldn't you?'

Jim shook his head and he Lottie walked back to the Land

Rover and got in, Lottie sitting up front in the passenger seat. Moments later, they were gone.

'Right, then,' said Lee, turning to me, 'let's get you sorted.'

We walked over to the other open stall, two down from Fancy's. Lee opened the bottom flap, ushered me in, came in behind me then closed both flaps. The darkness was sudden and total. Lee flicked a switch somewhere and an overhead strip bulb flickered noisily into life. The stall was square, warm and panelled, with a thick layer of sawdust covering the floor. There was a feeder trough affixed to one of the walls. It looked to be made of galvanised steel and had a visible waterline. While I was busy familiarising myself with the surroundings, Lee started sweeping back the sawdust with his foot and eventually uncovered a trap door. Crouching down, he unbolted it, swung it open and said, 'Excuse the smell. No-one's been down there for a bit.'

I peered over his shoulder and saw a wooden staircase leading down to what looked like a cave. It was dark and I could feel the cold from where I stood.

'What's down there?' I asked.

'We use it for storage,' said Lee, brushing the sawdust from his hand. 'Place is full of junk. Used to be an air raid shelter.'

I didn't think I suffered from claustrophobia until I saw that opening.

'After you,' said Lee, moving aside.

'No, please,' I replied, 'you first.'

Lee grinned and, leaning against the sides, eased himself into the gap. It was such a narrow, steep staircase that he had to climb down backwards. Once he was out of view, I took a deep breath and went down myself.

Lee hadn't exaggerated about the junk. The dim, naked lightbulb wasn't strong enough to pick out all the items, but I saw a lot of household appliances, stacks of boxes sagging under their weight and garden furniture of almost every description. Beyond the stored items, the shelter was in darkness. Lee told me later that the family used to run a DIY store until a B&Q opened up nearby and put them out of business.

The musty smell, the low ceiling that made it almost impossible to stand upright, the dim lighting, the piles of junk: no sane person would go willingly to such a place and then, having gone there, linger. I wanted out of there as soon as possible and it seemed Lee was of the same mind. 'Let's get this over with.' He opened the bingo bag and took out a handgun and then, moments later, a box of what I took to be bullets, even though the box was unmarked. Seeing the gun up close made my heart skip a beat. Lee weighed it in his hand, almost lovingly, then tried to hand it to me but I shrank back.

'Is it loaded?'

'No. I'll show you how to do that in a bit but for now I just want you to get a feel for it.'

I took the gun from him and, following his earlier example, weighed it in my hand. It was heavier than I'd expected. I gripped the worn handle and put my finger in the trigger holder. What happened next took me completely by surprise. The gun might not have been loaded but the mere idea of it made me feel powerful, fearless, invincible.

Lee said, 'Feels good, right?'

I didn't respond, too busy fantasising about what I was going to do Django.

Lee allowed me to indulge the feeling for a while then gently took the gun out of my hand and said, 'This, my friend, is a Browning 9mm semi-automatic. A classic of its kind.'

For the next half-hour or so, he gave me a lesson in its use and maintenance. He taught me how to operate the safety catch, how to open and close the chamber, how to remove and load the magazine, how to disassemble and reassemble the parts and how best to clean and lubricate them. He even gave me advice on how to store the gun, suggesting that I keep it in a cool dry place. That tickled me.

'You make it sound like a bag of rice.'

He laughed and said, 'So, you ready to test this baby or what?'

I broke out in a cold sweat. The big moment had arrived. I was about to fire a gun for the first time and, like a boy about to lose his virginity, I'd be lying if I said I wasn't nervous. As part of his instructions, Lee had loaded the magazine and had been very careful not to hand it back to me after that. I was a novice and he was being extra careful. When he did hand me the gun, he made sure to positon himself behind me. He actually put his arms around me and fastened both his hands onto both of mine. He said it was to help me with my aim but I got the feeling it was part of his safety precautions. At such close quarters, his aftershave was almost suffocating.

'Now, then. You see that box, the one marked Dunlopillo? Aim for the D. Use your sights if necessary.'

I closed one eye and squinted through the sights along the barrel.

'When you're ready, just squeeze the trigger. It's as simple as that.'

I waited a moment, trying desperately to steady my nerves, embarrassed at the idea that Lee could feel my hands shaking. The box was about ten feet away. I couldn't miss it but I wanted to hit the target. When I had it in my sights, I took a deep breath and squeezed. The noise almost deafened me, the recoil sent a shudder through my entire body and I actually jumped when I saw the empty shell fly out of the barrel to my right.

Even Lee rocked backwards but he held on to me and said, 'Again.'

With my ears still ringing, I planted my feet a little more firmly and fired off another round. The same deafening report, the same bone-juddering recoil, the empty shell flew out at the same height and speed, but this time I had anticipated them. I had blown two neat holes into the box, about ten inches apart, but only edged the target. I thought about the holes I was going to put into Django and my heart started pumping, a mixture of excitement and fear. The act itself, firing the gun, was a bit of an anti-climax. It was actually quite easy, but I got goosebumps from seeing the damage I'd caused to that box. Of course the real test was still to come. It was all very well firing bullets into an inanimate object: could I do the same thing to a human being, who might be firing back?

'Not bad,' said Lee. 'You've a good arm on you, steady. You need that with a beast like this.'

Carefully, and still standing behind me, he took the gun out of my hand, removed the magazine from the handle and took out the remaining bullets. He carefully slotted the bullets back into their box and then dropped the box, and the gun, into the bingo bag and tightened the string around the neck.

'By rights you should get some more practise in, but bullets cost a few bob and are hard to come by, so go easy.' He handed me the bag.

'Like I said, get it back to me when you're done.' And that was it. Not once had he mentioned what I was planning to do, or when. He didn't want to know, which suited me fine.

We climbed out of the shelter, hardly speaking. Lee closed the trapdoor and used his foot to re-cover it with sawdust. The horse stall felt luxurious compared to the dark dismal dungeon we'd just left. Back in the yard, Fancy was nowhere to be seen. I wondered if Lee's sister had come to get her and taken her for a ride somewhere. I almost asked Lee, but didn't because he had become pre-occupied with getting back to Dagenham to 'see a bloke about a bit of business'. When we got to his car, I suddenly realised that I would have to bring the gun back to London on public transport. In my panic I mentioned this to Lee and he told me not to worry. He said if I didn't mind waiting while he had his meeting, which he said wouldn't last more than an hour, he'd be happy to give me a lift back to Hackney. I didn't need to think twice about his offer.

When I got home that afternoon, Beverly said, 'Where've you been?'

'Round the squat?'

'Till now?'

'Yeah.'

'Doing what?'

'Just kicking it.'

'I thought you hated it round there now.'

'Please, Bev. I ain't in the mood.'

She was sitting in her usual spot, on the black, two-seater, fake-leather settee she'd bought from a second-hand furniture shop in Lower Clapton. She had the black-and-white TV on with the volume down to avoid disturbing Shereen, who was asleep on her lap, sucking her thumb. She was always complaining about bills but had the heating on full blast in early September.

I walked over to the window, stepping over Shereen's dolls along the way, noticing that the thin grey carpet had a stain that hadn't been there when I left that morning. The wind up on the twelfth floor was murder, so noisy and so strong it actually swayed the block, but I had to crack the window a little bit as it was just too hot and stuffy in the room. It wasn't possible to open it any wider because the windows had been installed to deter the tenants from jumping to their deaths. The flats used to be known for suicides and the council had been forced by the residents to do something. Many a child, and not a few adults, had been traumatised over the years by the sight of bodies lying splattered in the courtyard.

When I opened the window, Beverly silently mouthed for me to shut it, but I ignored her. I knew she couldn't get up without waking Shereen so I stood there looking out across the city, admiring the incredible view while thinking over what I had been doing that morning. It all seemed so disconnected from my life in Hackney: the Essex countryside, the horse-stalls, Fancy, Jim and his dog Lottie, the air-raid shelter, and, of course, Lee and his lessons on how to use a gun. I was trying to process it all when I remembered that I was standing by the window with the bingo bag still in my hand. I immediately closed the window and, to stop any bad feeling from developing between us, went over and kissed Beverly then went out to the bathroom to find a place to hide the gun.

I hit it behind the panel at the side of the bathtub, a flimsy piece of plywood that fell in if you so much as blew on it. To make sure Beverly didn't find the bag by accident I got down on my belly and shoved it as far back against the wall as possible, inhaling a load of dust in the process. And even then I wasn't happy. The thought of what she would say or do if she discovered that I'd brought a gun into the house where she lived with her baby didn't bear thinking about. It was wrong of me and I felt guilty but I had to store the thing somewhere. I decided to take a bath. It might have been my imagination but I thought I could smell the air-raid shelter on my clothes.

While I soaked, I thought some more about the time I had just spent with Lee. He was a funny one. He didn't want me asking a lot of questions but had put me in a position where it was only natural for me to do so. For instance, what was the nature of his relationship with Jim? The man was obviously some kind of farmer, he obviously lived close to the land but was he also a villain? He had brought the gun out to Lee so was probably an armourer for hire. Had he met Theodore? Had Theodore been to the stables for shooting practise? Had Theodore met Fancy or Lee's sister? So many questions; a lot of them to do with my brother's former life, the one he had before he became a crack-head. Had Lee and the other gang members tried to do anything to stop him from taking drugs? He was like a brother to them, according to Lee, so they must have been saddened to see how he turned out, the way he had almost destroyed himself with drugs. Had they tried to intervene in any way, offered to pay for him to have treatment or anything like that? I should have asked Lee about it and I kicked myself for not doing so. I couldn't put my finger on why, but it felt like a missed opportunity of some kind.

With the bath running cold, I added some more hot water and continued to soak, half thinking, half-sleeping. At one point Beverly came to the door and tried to come in but I had locked it. 'You gonna be in there all day?' She didn't sound annoyed, more concerned, as if she thought I was trying to drown myself. 'I'll be out in a while.' She went silent and then I heard her footfalls as she loped back along the lino to the living room.

Since the attack on Theodore she had become almost motherly towards me, constantly worried that I was going to do something foolish. She had consistently urged me to let the police deal with the matter and thought I'd be mad to show my face on the Front again. The truth was, Theodore getting stabbed had shaken her up in a way that she hadn't expected. When she heard what had happened, she cried for hours. When she first saw him in hospital, I had to escort her out of the ward. She couldn't bear to look at him. Theodore had become a part of her, he had touched her in a way that she hadn't thought possible when he first moved in looking and smelling like an animal. She had lived with him for over six months, had shared things with him, intimate things, she had been a sister to him, a mother, a friend. She had grown to love him. The fact that he had come so close to death had left her half out of her mind with fear, too afraid even to leave the flat. Always a homebody, she had now become a virtual recluse. It was rare for her to be out after dark and she could never relax until she heard me putting my key in the door. And once I was in, she would do everything to make sure I stayed in. If we ran out of anything and I offered to go down and get it from our local corner shop, she'd plead with me to leave it till the morning. She would sooner wrap Shereen in a tea towel than send me out at night to get nappies. She began to see dangers and threats everywhere and was now talking about making a change.

It hadn't been two days since Theodore's attack when she announced that if she could wrangle it somehow, she'd move out of Hackney. 'And go where?' I asked. She paused for a moment then said, 'Somewhere out of London. Somewhere a person can breathe. The countryside maybe.' I laughed and said, 'The countryside? Yeah, right.' I dismissed the idea, and kept slapping it down every time she brought it up, but in truth I could see where she was coming from, especially since she had a child to raise. The problem for her was that she had so few options. She could dream, but to make that dream a reality, for someone in her position, was next to impossible.

* * *

I wouldn't say I no longer feared Django but having that gun had definitely lessened my fear. The odds had been evened up considerably. I had given myself a chance to come out of the thing on top. But one questioned remained: five days after he had been stabbed, was I still as committed to avenging Theodore? The answer, when it came right down to it, was

132

no. The intensity of the feeling had decreased, aided by my conversations with Beverly. But if she was the voice of my conscience, Mitch was my avenging angel.

The day after my trip to Dagenham he and Benjy came by to see me at home. He told me that Django had been bragging on the Front about stabbing Theodore and had sworn to do the same to me if and when he saw me. I had no reason to disbelieve Mitch but still I made Benjy confirm it.

'It's true, Si. He's been beating his gums about what he's gonna do to you.'

'Yeah,' said Mitch. 'He's taking you for a pussy.'

We'd been talking outside on the landing, to avoid being overheard by Beverly, but she was no fool. She knew what we were discussing and came out to speak her mind. Directing her comments at Mitch, she said, 'Why won't you stop? Eh? You trying to get him killed? Is that it? He's too damn weak to tell you, so I'm telling you. Go away. Leave us alone. Simon ain't got nothing to prove. Theodore's alive. End of.'

Mitch tried to say something but Beverly put her hand in his face and said, 'No, Mitch! I don't wanna hear no more of your shit. Go away. Right now. You too Benjy. And I beg you, don't come back.'

Mitch looked at me, pleadingly, but I couldn't do anything for him. He said, 'Come, Benj. Let's dust. We know who wears the trousers round here.'

Benjy said, 'Mitch, man, why you gotta talk shegries all the time.'

Mitch kissed his teeth and walked off. Benjy watched him go then turned to me and said, 'Si, look. Don't feel no way, I ain't trying to tell you what to do. If you wanna let this t'ing slide, that's all good with me. Man and man is bredren, no matter what.'

He put up his fist, I punched it and he said, 'Catch you on the reverb.'

After a quick nod at Beverly, he bounced off down the narrow, strip-lit landing towards the lift. Beverly pulled me inside. We went and sat in the living room and for the next hour or so, I listened while she made quite a convincing case as to why I should cut Mitch and Benjy out of my life. I say I listened but in fact my mind was on Django. The old heat was rising again. Beverly went on and on until eventually she realised I was daydreaming, 'Are you even listening to me?' I didn't answer. I didn't want to talk to her. I sat and stared at Shereen, who was in her playpen, gurgling and trying to bite one of her plastic toys. Her features were starting to form, the resemblance to her father was starting to show.

Eventually Beverly said, 'Oh go to hell, then.' She leapt up, grabbed Shereen from the playpen and stormed out. Moments later I heard the bedroom door slam. I didn't move or react in any way. My mind was racing but I was showing no outward signs of agitation. There were no shakes and my breathing was even and quiet. A lot of words had been spoken in the last hour so. Beverly had said her piece, Benjy had gone out of his way to reassure me of his friendship, but as I sat there on the settee staring at my reflection in the TV screen, it was Mitch's words that sounded the loudest. 'He's taking you for a pussy.' Slowly, deliberately, I got up and went out to the bathroom.

It was a Tuesday night, just after nine. There was a slight chill in the air, made worse by a slight drizzle. The street lamps, those that worked, cast wide pools of amber light all along the road. The lamps were very bright, had been made that way to deter dealing, but most of that was taking place in the dark spaces between. As per usual for that time of night, the police presence had been scaled back to a couple of sentries, one at either end of the road, leaving the side roads unattended. I had used one of these roads – Montague – to creep up unseen.

In the entrance to the alley that ran behind the Lord Stanley pub, which stood on the corner of Sandringham and Montague, I had positioned myself to observe the goings on. This was supposed to be my patch and yet there I was skulking about in an alley like a rat. I felt sorry myself and desperately alone. My position gave me an angled view of the main drag, where most of the people were standing around in groups. There was quite a bit of noise, mostly shouted conversations as people competed with one another to be heard above the general din. Everything about the scene felt unfamiliar, strange, not quite as I had remembered it. In less than a week my view of the world seemed to have altered. Nothing made sense any more. I didn't know where I was, who I was or what I was doing. I wanted to run away, far away, and never come back, but at the same time I knew I would never know any peace until I had settled my account with Django. The thought that he'd been bragging about stabbing my brother and threatening to do the same to me, made me want to punch the wall. The moment he popped into my head my heartbeat quickened. Instinctively I reached round and felt the gun in my waist. The cold steel pressed against my skin felt reassuring.

I couldn't see him. Some of his crew were there, most of them in fact, but I couldn't see him. I stared and stared, hoping to spot him, praying that I hadn't shown up on the one night when he wasn't around. And then, as it from nowhere, he suddenly appeared. He'd been there all along, but out of view, urinating behind a parked transit van. I knew this because when he emerged he was still doing up his flies. This time, instead of feeling for the gun, I pulled it out of my waist and eased off the safety catch. I still didn't know exactly how I wanted to play the thing, but by removing the safety I felt as if I'd moved to the next stage, edged a little closer to the precipice.

I watched and waited, looking for a chink. Django and his boys stood around doing what they always did: chatting, drinking bottles of Dragon Stout, rolling and smoking spliffs. Occasionally, one of them would break off from the group to sell a bit of crack to a junkie but mostly they remained together, safety in numbers. An hour passed. It felt more like five. Finally, at around ten thirty, people started drifting away. The activity and noise levels fell noticeably. At eleven, from my position behind the Lord Stanley, I heard the bell for last orders. This made me move a little further down the alley, a little further into the darkness, to avoid the exiting punters. By eleven thirty the pub had emptied. Several people walked past the alley into Montague Road, but none saw me. The alley was too dark.

Once I saw the lights go off in the back of pub and heard the doors being bolted, I came back to the mouth of the alley and peered across the road to see what the Yardies were doing. Only two of them remained. Fleas (Django's unacknowledged second) and Django himself. I continued to wait, pacing about and tapping the gun against my leg until I remembered that the safety was off. I put it back on but kept the gun in my hand. I was getting impatient and at one point I had an urge to run up on them and start blasting way but I composed myself. I had waited that long; a little longer wouldn't doing any harm and would probably make all the difference. The element of surprise was crucial. I didn't doubt for a minute that Django was armed and I knew I couldn't afford to give him space and time to act.

People continued to drift away but not Django or Fleas. I couldn't understand it. What the hell were they up to? The Front was dead. Most people had left. Anyone looking to buy a draw or any junkies on the hunt for crack had now moved on to other watering holes in the area. And yet Django and Fleas, and the handful of other dealers, were still milling about as if they had no homes to go. I was becoming frantic, my heart pounding, my breath now coming in short, erratic bursts. I needed a release, I needed something to happen and soon. And finally it did. At around a quarter to midnight, after a wait of almost three hours, I saw Django and Fleas touch fists and go off in opposite directions. Django took the first left into Amhurst Road but I couldn't go after him. I had to hold my position because Fleas was walking directly towards me. I watched him cross the road and felt certain that he had seen me and that he and Django had devised a plan to circle me. I quickly glanced over my shoulder to try to see if Django was even then coming up behind me, but it was too dark. I gripped the gun and eased myself further into the alley, close enough

137

to the mouth to see what Fleas was doing and but also looking behind me in case Django suddenly appeared. With my back against the wall and both hands on the gun, I was getting ready to blast whichever one of them got to me first.

I'd been panicking for nothing. Like those punters who had come out of the Lord Stanley earlier, Fleas walked straight past the alley into Montague Road and within seconds had rounded the bend out of sight. I was standing no more than ten feet from him but he hadn't seen me. Once he was out of view, I sprinted out of the alley on to the Front and flew down towards Amhurst Road, the gun in my hand, the safety off again. There were still some people standing around on the Front but I ran past them in a blur, too quick for them to register it was me.

Django had had quite a head start on me and I knew I'd have to go some to catch up with him. By the time I turned into Amhurst Road he was nowhere to be seen. My heart sank. I carried on running, desperately looking left and right and peering ahead into the distance. And then I spotted him, about a hundred yards ahead. He was standing still, seemed to fishing around in his pocket for something. I slowed down, started walking, mindful not to get too close. The road was deserted except for the odd passing vehicle. I eased myself behind a parked car, crouched down and peeped out to see what he was doing. He found what he was looking for. The keys to his car. I'd forgotten he had one, a broken down Ford Fiesta. He was standing next to it, about to put the key in the driver's door. To avoid missing my opportunity, I leapt to my feet and started jogging towards him, not caring now if he saw me, committed, with only one thing on my mind. At the last moment he sensed me approaching and was about to turn around but he was too late: I shot him once in the back of the head. He collapsed like a felled tree and didn't move again or make a sound. I had a quick look around. I felt breathless, my heart was pounding, I was trembling so much I thought my legs would buckle. I stared down at Django, at his already vacant eyes, at the odd angle of his legs, at the blood oozing from the hole in his head. I felt nothing for him, no more than if I'd squashed a fly. Suddenly aware that the gun was still in my hand, I shoved it down my waist. The muzzle was so hot it burnt my skin. I had another look around. This time I saw a few curtains twitching, and several houses that were in darkness moments earlier now had lights on. And then, all at once, with a force that made me giddy, I was hit by the full horror of what I'd done. I turned and sprinted away.

When I got home, at around one thirty, Beverly had already gone to bed. To avoid disturbing her or Shereen, I crept to the bathroom, hid the gun under the bath, removed my clothes and dumped them in the wash basket. On impulse, I had a quick shower, put on my bathrobe that was hanging on the back of the door, then crept out to the kitchen. From the cupboard I pulled out a half bottle of Martell brandy and took several gulps. It had no effect so I went to the living room and rolled a spliff. The effects of the two, the weed and the brandy, soon kicked in, made me feel woozy, but didn't stop me from thinking about what I'd just done. Short of a lobotomy, I couldn't imagine a time when I'd ever stop thinking about it. I kept seeing Django's eyes as the life drained out of him.

The guilt and remorse I felt was almost suffocating.

Unable to keep still, I paced up and down. The room was so small and cramped I couldn't vary my movements; now to the window, now to the settee, now back to the window. I felt like a caged animal. It didn't help that the curtains were drawn. I went over to the window and pulled them apart and stood there for a moment staring out at the views. They didn't seem as impressive as the day before. I cracked the top pane of the window and, just for a minute, rued the fact that the main part had been sealed. Would I have jumped? Probably not but I definitely thought about it. I kept pacing, sucking on my spliff and swigging from the brandy bottle. Eventually I felt the adrenalin starting to wear off and then, in an instant, I crashed. I'd never felt as tired in my life, not even when I used to play football three times a week. I slumped on to the settee and within minutes was fast asleep. I don't know how long I was out but when Beverly woke me up, the room was bright with sunlight.

Immediately I covered my eyes and begged Beverly to draw the curtains, but all she said was, 'What the hell you gone and done?' I sat up, my head as heavy as a bag of sand, then staggered out to the kitchen and poured myself a glass of water and stood at the sinking gulping it down. I couldn't remember water ever tasting so good. Beverly had followed me. Still wearing her nightgown, she stood in the doorway, her arms folded around her stomach, her eyes puffy with sleep. 'Well?' she said. There was fear in her voice. 'Shereen still asleep?' I asked, stalling for time. 'Never mind her,' said Beverly, 'just answer my question.' I told her. She let me get it all out then shook her head and said, 'You just couldn't leave it could you?'

Django didn't die. He lost the use of an eye and an arm and his speech would never be the same again, but, incredibly, he'd survived. He spent over a month in hospital and then, when they thought he was fit enough to travel, the police deported him back to Jamaica to face charges of multiple homicide. It came out, in the *Hackney Gazette*, that his real name was Sonny Renton and that he'd been on the run from the Jamaican authorities for years, as was the case with a lot of the Yardies who arrived in London in the eighties, but whilst it was a slight comfort to know that he was no longer around, I still had to deal with his friends.

Fleas had made it his personal mission to put me down. I heard from Mitch that he was getting so impatient to have his revenge that he had promised to pay for information leading to my whereabouts. I may have been afraid for my life, but I was not so cowed into terror that I couldn't recognise the humour in the situation. Behind his back, Fleas was called Ladbroke, with the emphasis very much on the 'broke'. There were days when he would take such a hammering in the bookies he could barely feed himself, let alone finance a vendetta against me. But his gambling addiction did not in any way detract from the fact that he was a heartless sonofabitch with the blood of many dead people on his hands. I was under no illusions about him. He had declared me as his next victim and that was as close to being given a death sentence as I was ever likely to come.

I had no choice but to go into hiding. Fortunately, that was not so difficult to do as I had the advantage over the Yardies of being a native Londoner. I knew the city in a way they never could. I moved out of Beverly's place and, through a friend of Ras Malachi's, wound up living in a tiny council sub-let in Edmonton. Not long after that Beverly moved in with her cousin south of the river and that was pretty much the end of us as a couple. I saw her a few more times, I went to visit her in Peckham, but the situation was impossible and we knew it. The last time we saw each other, she told me she had met someone from the area and that they were planning on moving out to the suburbs, to Sutton, which apparently had very good schools. 'I want to give Shereen a chance.'

While all this had been happening, Theodore had had a spiritual awakening. Within a few weeks of leaving hospital he had become a born-again Christian. He started going to his local Pentecostal church every Sunday and became something of a poster boy for their ongoing work to rescue young black men from a life of drugs and crime. His transformation left me astonished. He had become a completely different person, recognisable to me in looks only. I tried to be understanding as I feared losing him again. It had happened once before, when he'd been running around with Lee and the rest of them, and now I was in danger of losing him to a different type of gang. The situation was becoming intolerable. The gap between us was just too wide and the day finally came when I decided to have it out with him.

Ironically, it happened on a Sunday. I went to see him in his one-bedroom flat in a converted Victorian terrace in Stoke Newington, which his church had financed. He wasn't working yet but was actively looking. The deal was that he'd pay the church back the deposit on the place and any rent he had accrued when eventually he found a job. They were looking after him, I had to give them that. The place was spacious and newly-decorated, but with just a bed, a dining table and two dining chairs, it was a long way from being homely and felt unfinished. There was sawdust on the window-frames and around the skirting boards and the smell of glue and varnish was everywhere. He had painted the place himself and not to a very high standard. The functional grey carpet, fitted in every room, was covered in spots of white paint. I couldn't help but tease him about his decorating skills. 'Remind me not to hire you to do my place.'

He had cooked. Chicken and rice and peas. He had always been a dab hand in the kitchen. Mum used to try and teach us but he had shown more attention, and aptitude, than me. I was about to start tucking in when he held his hand up and said, 'In this house we say grace before we eat.' With the fork poised in front of my mouth, I looked at him as if he was joking, but the expression in his eyes and the set of his mouth said otherwise. Angrily, I dropped the fork on to my plate and watched as he clasped his hands, bowed his head, closed his eyes and said, 'The only sustenance that matters, Lord, comes from you. For all that you provide for us – the food on our table, the roof over our heads, the clothes on our backs, health, strength and vitality – we give thanks.' I thought he'd never shut up. I had arrived at his place with the hunger of three men, but in the end I only managed half of what was on my plate. His condescending attitude had robbed me of my appetite.

Just this once I was determined not to be preached at and did everything I could to avoid it. I talked about football, which he loved as much as me. I went all nostalgic and recounted some of the happier moments from our childhood, such as the time when our aunt Viola gave us full cowboy outfits for Christmas presents, complete with Stetsons, gun belts and two six shooters apiece. I loved mine so much I wore it all the time, even in bed. I reminded him of the first girl he ever had a crush on, Samantha Braithwaite, who let him feel her up one day in our bedroom when she came by with her mother, a friend of dad's from Jamaica. I mentioned the year he and I went to Butlins with our local boys club and how he loved it so much he cried when we had to go home. I knew that would get to him. For years afterwards he would talk about that holiday and he did on this occasion, too.

'Remember the song they were playing when that girl came up to you in the disco and kissed you on the cheek?'

'Dancing Queen,' he replied. He stared down at his plate, turning the rice over with his fork, transported, momentarily, back to Bognor Regis, 1976. I had him right where I wanted him and was keen to keep him there.

'Ever wonder what became of her?' I asked.

He nodded and said, 'Now and then. I remember she said she was from Sussex. Eastbourne in Sussex. I've never been there but the way she described it…' he became thoughtful again, then went on, '…I wonder if she still lives there.'

And then he began to preach. I was naïve to think I'd escaped. It was a Sunday, after all, and he'd been at church all morning and most of the afternoon.

'Why won't you come to church, Simon?'

'Damn, bruv! We were doing so well.'

'Seriously, I wish you would.'

'And I wish you wouldn't.'

I stood up and started gathering up the empty dishes.

'Sit down, Simon. Let's talk. We used to be able to talk. I miss that.'

I sat down again, a frown on my face. I could feel him looking at me, but I didn't want to meet his eyes. Instead I turned my head away and focussed on a spot on the bare white wall, thinking how it could use a picture of some kind, or a mirror. A space as big as that was just begging to be covered up.

'I worry about you, Simon. I really do. You're not a kid any more. You're seventeen years old, soon to be eighteen. Don't you think its time you grew up and faced a few facts.'

'What you chatting about, 'facts'?'

'Well, number one, you have to change the way you're living.'

'Says who?'

I heard him sigh, shift about in his seat. 'Answer me this,' he said, 'do you think it's right that you haven't been to see Mum and Dad in months? It's not right, Simon. I know because I used to treat them the same way, remember? But I see now how wrong I was. No matter how badly I thought of them, they're still my parents and I should have had the decency to honour them. I tell you, making things up with Dad is one of the best things I ever did.'

I turned and stared at him and was surprised to see that he had welled up a bit. Embarrassed, he suddenly stood up and went out to the kitchen. I heard him rattling around, heard the clink of glasses, the familiar suction sound of a fridge door opening and closing again. He was right about our parents. I had been avoiding them and for the same reasons I'd been avoiding him. They had used Theodore's conversion to Christianity as a stick to beat me with.

'Why you don't do like yuh bredda and go to church?'

I detested their hypocrisy. For all their seeming devoutness, I couldn't remember the last time either of them had set foot inside a church. It really galled me to have to take lectures from them on the matter of my salvation, but at the end of the day they were my parents and so I had to suck it up. In any case, their badgering was kind of reassuring. It meant they hadn't completely written me off. I could have done without their lecturing, but I preferred that to them washing their hands of me.

Theodore came back in looking more composed, with two tall glasses filled with what I immediately recognised as Guinness punch. 'There's ice if you want it, but it should be cold enough. It's been in the fridge since last night.' He came over and put one of the glasses in front of me and went back to his chair. I took a sip. Not like Mum's, a bit too much nutmeg and not sweet enough, but good.

'Listen,' he said, 'I only say what I say to you out of love. I know you think I'm a joke, I know you don't have any respect for me...'

I had to cut in there. 'That ain't true, Theodore. It ain't true and it ain't fair of you to say it. I do respect you.'

'You do?'

'Of course I do.'

'You have a funny way of showing it. Is it respectful to show up here with a loaded gun bulging in your waist?

146

I stared at him, weighing my response carefully. I was prepared to concede the point but before that I had some truths of my own that needed airing.

'You got a short memory, Theodore. Who looked after you when you were cracked out? Me. Who came to visit you three times a day in hospital when you were this close...' I squeezed my forefinger and thumb together, '...to going out? Me. And I haven't even mentioned Django yet. He puts more holes in you than a grater, leaves you for dead, then starts bragging about it. Who put it on that faggot? Was it God? No. I did that. So please, don't talk to me about love and respect, bruv. We can all talk about that.'

After that we really got into it. He used his tried and trusted argument about God working in mysterious ways.

'We don't know. Maybe it was part of his divine plan that I got stabbed. I certainly believe I've been given a second chance, a chance to do some good in the world.'

I wasn't having any of it. 'You can do good in the world without being a God freak.'

'I'm not a freak. If you're going to insult me you can leave right now.'

We got even deeper into it, to'ing and fro'ing, pulling and tugging at each other like we used to do as kids. Try as I did, I couldn't make him see that he was being a fool, that he had been brainwashed by people who prey on the vulnerable for their own self-serving ends.

'What you on about, Simon? I'm not part of some cult. Nobody brainwashed me. I told you, Christ visited me in hospital. In person. He sat down beside me and spoke to me. He brought me back to life. It's down to Him that I'm sitting here with you today. No, bruv. If anyone's been brainwashed, it's you.'

At last we fell silent. We'd talked ourselves out, used up all our energy. I wasn't sure how he felt, but I thought something good had happened, some obstacle that had been standing between us had now been removed or at least shifted to one side. That's what I was thinking but I had second thoughts when Theodore said, 'To go back to Django. Two wrongs don't make a right. You have to repent. I can't stress that enough. You have to accept that what you did was wicked and ask the Almighty to forgive you.'

I didn't know what. After that the silence sat between us at the table like a wino; rude, uninvited, smelly. Eventually, for something to say, I praised the cooking and offered to do the washing up.

'We can do it together,' he said. 'I'll wash, you can dry.'

'Deal.'

He started gathering up the dishes and I went to the toilet. I needed to go but when I got there I decided to hide the gun and pick it up on my way out. After what Theodore had said earlier, it seemed liked the least I should do. At first I didn't know where to put it. I tried to wedge it behind the cistern but it wasn't concealed enough. In the end I hid it in the boiler cupboard then went to join Theodore in the kitchen. We washed the dishes in silence.

* * *

I continued to hide out, coming into Hackney only to sign on and to cash my giro cheques. The rest of the time I spent cooling my heels in Edmonton. To supplement my income I started selling a bit of hash from my flat to a bunch of white kids who lived on my estate and who smoked the stuff as if it was going out of fashion. To earn the money to support their habit they had turned their local area into a virtual crime zone. They must have broken into every car, house and shop within a five mile radius of the estate. Their parents, those who weren't banged up, had allowed them to run so wild they had become almost feral. They hated everyone who tried to come between them and their freedom to do whatever the hell they wanted. They especially hated the police, and as I had no love for the Met' myself, I could relate to them if only on that score. They took a real liking to me. Not only because I always had good hash – they had a particular weakness for Lebanese Brown and I would go out of my way to try and get it for them – but also because I was black.

It was for kids like these that the word 'wigga' was coined. Their clothes, the language they used, the music they listened to, even their hopes and dreams; all of it was influenced by black culture, and specifically Jamaican culture. This one wanted a black girlfriend who wore nothing but batty-riders, that one wanted as fearsome a rep as a Yardie, another wanted to go to Jamaica to smoke Sensi all day, every day. They were utterly ridiculous. But I liked them. So much so that I allowed them to have the run of my flat. Most evenings they would assemble in my front room to smoke hash till late into the night. In return for my hospitality and generosity they gave me their loyalty and even their love. They couldn't do enough for me. If they went out on the thieve, I got first refusal on their ill-gotten gains. When Old Bill came snooping about, they acted as my early-warning system. They had my back. They looked up to me. They

149

also feared me. It was important that they did and I made sure of it by regularly brandishing the Browning. At the sight of it they'd become, quite literally, dumbstruck. Whenever they made me angry – which was often – I would shout and threaten them and wave the gun about and send them scurrying for the door like so many rats fleeing a larder. I didn't like to frighten them in this way but I had to do it from time to time to keep them in check. After my bouts of anger they would give me a wide berth for a few days, but then slowly, one by one, they would drift back and things would return to normal.

Living as a kind of exile in the back of beyond, playing Fagin to a gang of juvenile crooks – and white ones to boot – was not my idea of a life. But then I couldn't see a realistic alternative. I might have yearned for a more honourable, more virtuous way of living but I couldn't picture it. I couldn't see beyond my immediate situation. The only thing I knew was that I didn't want to be on the run any more. I was fed up of hiding. I had to do something to bring the situation to a close.

* * *

Dealing from my flat was always going to attract the attention of the police, but I did it in the hope that when they came calling I would receive enough warning from my scouts to be able to get rid of whatever I was holding. It didn't turn out that way, not exactly. On the day the police smashed in my door, I got the heads up soon enough to be able to hurl my block of hash and the gun out the back window of my fifth-floor flat, but in my haste I'd forgotten the bag of weed in my bedroom. Fortunately it was only small, half an ounce of prime red-beard Ses, so when I appeared in court a few weeks later it was on the lesser charge of 'possession' and not the much more serious 'possession with intent to supply'. I pleaded guilty and was fined two hundred and fifty quid and given a six-month suspended sentence. I thought it was a bit harsh, but at least I had walked out of court. The fact that I now had a criminal record was almost a minor consideration.

I got my hash and gun back. I had written them off as lost, but even as I was being handcuffed one of my boys had sneaked round the back of the flats and picked them up for safe keeping. For his initiative I rewarded him with an eighth of Leb and a lot of praise.

After the first raid, the police came back twice in quick succession. On both occasions they came up empty-handed – my scouts had been put on extra alert and posted at all the estate's main entrances – but I knew it was only a question of time before they got me. I felt it was time to move on but I had nowhere else to go. I was paying a slightly higher rent than the council were charging the registered tenant, but it was still quite cheap. I couldn't imagine where I would find such a cushy number again. I didn't even bother considering the private rental market. Even if I'd had the necessary papers – references and bank statements and such – I couldn't have afforded the extortionate deposit. I might have been dealing, but that didn't mean I was rolling in dough. In American parlance, I was a nickle-and-dimer, a low-level hash dealer who still relied on his giro as a way to supplement his income. For all those reasons,

151

I was extremely reluctant to give up my sub-let. I wanted to leave, it made sense for me to leave, but until I had something else lined up, something as cheap or cheaper, I had to stay put. It was a case of needs must.

When I heard a high-ranking Met' officer describe the Yardies as 'a cancer that must not be allowed to take hold in Britain', I began to see a way out of my situation. The officer, who was being interviewed on TV after a shooting incident in Stockwell, went on to say, 'It would be remiss of us as police officers to underestimate the threat posed to society by these gangs and I want to reassure the public that we are not underestimating it.' The police had to do something, or at least be seen to be doing something. And so, where in the early eighties the Yardies had been tolerated, by the middle of the decade they were being routinely arrested and deported, or 'dipped' as we used to say. I practically sat on my hands and waited to hear news that Fleas and his crew had been rounded up and sent home, but, depressingly, none came. They were obviously not high enough on the list of Jamaica's most wanted, but even so, the police clearly had them on the run. Whilst not exactly living underground – there were too many haunts in the London where they could congregate without disturbance – they didn't dare show their faces on the Front. For me, that represented progress, but it didn't draw me out of hiding, not completely. I sneaked on to the Front occasionally, but only when I had received word from either Mitch or Benjy that the coast was clear and only for a few minutes at a time. The situation had improved, I could breathe a little easier, but my life was still very much in danger.

The police finally got me. One night, on my way home, I got pounced on by a gang of plain clothes CID boys. They raided my flat and found my stash of hash but, by a stroke of pure luck, not the gun. At the station, under questioning, I realised I'd been grassed up and that the snake was probably one of my boys. 'Where's the gun, Simon? Where have you hidden it?' I hadn't hidden it. A mere two days before I was arrested I had given it back to Lee who said he needed it for 'a job' and that I could borrow it again just as soon as he had finished with it. The police had been foiled in their primary objective and were not happy about it at all. Under normal circumstances, a charge of 'possession with intent to supply' would have been a result for them, but in my case they regarded that as second prize. For the amount of hash they'd found, I was probably looking at a measly eighteen months inside, whereas with the gun, I might have expected something closer to five years.

In the end I left the sub-let not through my own choice, but because the police forced the council to evict me and board the place up until such time as the new tenants moved in. Actually, technically speaking, it wasn't me they evicted but the person whose identity I'd been using. I hadn't told him I was dealing from his flat and when he found out he'd lost the place he blew his top and had a go at Ras Malachi who in turn had a go at me. There was nothing I could do to make things up except offer a bit of money – five hundred pounds – which the tenant grudgingly accepted. As to my boys, I turned my back on them without so much as a backward glance. I was so incensed at the thought that one of them had grassed me up that I decided to stay well away from them in case I did something I would end up regretting.

During my summary appearance at Highbury Corner Magistrates Court, the police had asked that I be remanded in custody to await my trial because of the seriousness of my offence and because I was now of 'no fixed abode', but on the basis of my previous court appearance my brief had argued that I was hardly a flight risk and that I should be granted unconditional bail. On the question of where I resided, he gave assurances to the court that I had moved back in with my parents and that they were even prepared to stand surety against the risk of me doing a runner. My parents had done no such thing. They didn't even know I'd been arrested, but I had sworn to my brief that they were in my corner and that they would do anything to help secure my release. Having listened carefully to both arguments, the Magistrates granted me bail, but made it clear that their decision had less to do with my solicitor's argument and more to do with their reluctance to add unnecessarily to the overcrowded prison population. And even then they only released me on condition that I report once a week to my local nick. It didn't matter to me what condition they imposed, because I had no intention of either reporting to the police or showing up for my trial. The moment I walked out of that courtroom I was effectively on the run, which meant that with Fleas on one side and the police on the other, I had no room for manoeuvre.

With nowhere left to turn, I moved back into the squat with Mitch and Benjy. I rarely went out. The squat was not exactly impregnable, but with all the security doors and burglar bars, Fleas would have had a hard time getting in. After showering me with praise for what I had done to Django, Mitch had turned on me for going into hiding. For him, the courage I had shown in avenging my brother had been completely undone by my subsequent behaviour. It goes without saying that I saw the situation in a different light. I believed I had done the sensible thing in the face of overwhelming odds, but to Mitch I was just being gutless. In my shoes, he would have launched an all-out attack on Fleas and his boys, given them, as he described it, 'pure agony'.

One day, soon after I had moved in with them, Benjy said, 'Let's kidnap the faggot, torture him, then give him the old Corleone treatment.' When I asked for an explanation of the 'Corleone treatment', Benjy said, 'We weigh the fucker down with cement and throw him in the Thames.' At this, Mitch bared his teeth, like a snarling Rottweiller. 'Yeah, yeah, and then we send a fish wrapped in newspaper to all his pussyhole friends. "Fleas sleeps with the fishes". Ha!' I found this sort of talk ludicrous, cartoonish, but I couldn't dismiss it because I knew that Mitch at least was being deadly serious. Schooled in films like *The Godfather* and *Scarface*, he was itching to act out his gangster fantasies and saw my situation with Fleas as the perfect opportunity to do so. I didn't even want to think about what they were suggesting, much less carry it out, but that was before I received news that Fleas and his boys, in a desperate attempt to flush me out of hiding, had fired shots through the window of my parents' flat.

To be a player, you had to observe the rules of the game. If you had a beef with someone, you sorted it privately. You never went to the police, you never involved civilians, and you never, ever targeted your enemy's parents. Fleas had crossed the line, and from that moment he was as good as dead in my eyes.

My parents didn't know who had attacked them, but they suspected it had something to do with me. I protested my innocence, strongly, but they were not persuaded. More angry than afraid, they ended up calling the police, who of course couldn't help them. An unprovoked attack without witnesses wasn't much for them to go on. They surmised that it was probably a case of mistaken identity and advised my parents to stay away from their flat for a while, just in case.

In films, the police always went further. They investigated, they interviewed friends and family and neighbours, they put the word out on the street to see if their informants could tell them anything, but this was real life, this was Hackney in the eighties, this was a crime involving a Black family. The case was closed before it had even been opened. A potentially deadly attack, committed with firearms, didn't seem to concern them over-much. They were more interested in tracking me down because I hadn't reported to the police station as stipulated under my bail agreement. After interviewing them over the shooting, they told my parents to inform me that there was now a warrant out for my arrest and that I should do the sensible thing and give myself up. There was no chance of me doing that. At that time all I could think about was how to hit back at Fleas. Now that I had Mitch and Benjy helping me out, I had made up my mind to take the fight to him. The game had changed. It was now me on the front foot.

My plan was to rub out Fleas and hope that the rest of his crew would become demoralised and scatter. I'd heard that their heart wasn't really in the fight, that they were only going along with Fleas out of fear, that one or two were even secretly hoping that I would do away with him and in this way remove his boot from their necks. They had come to England to escape the gangster way of life. Like most immigrants, they had come to work hard and make money to send back to their suffering relatives in Jamaica. They were more than happy to exploit their fearsome reputations as and when it suited them, but had little interest in waging a long-running war with an enemy they couldn't see, on a battleground they didn't know. What had happened to Django had exposed their vulnerability. And with the police now harassing them at every turn, the word on the street was that they were fed up. They wanted out of a country they had initially regarded as a soft touch – in comparison to the States – but which had proved to be anything but. In fact, a couple of Fleas' gang had already departed for calmer shores – Canada of all places – and others were rumoured to be thinking of joining them. But until then, they were stuck with Fleas. If this was indeed an accurate assessment of the situation – and I had enough eyes and ears on the street to assure me that it was – then my goal was simple. Get Fleas.

Mitch was in his element. He spent a lot of time and energy discussing what methods of torture he would use against Fleas and how he would bring him to such heights of pain that he would end up begging to be killed. I just wanted the guy dead, quickly and without fuss, but I had to let Mitch have his pound of flesh if I wanted his help. As for Benjy, he was happy to go along with whatever. He wasn't exactly making up the numbers, I knew that if we got into a jam he wouldn't be found wanting, but he was not and had never been as vicious or vindictive as Mitch. He wasn't after blood for the sake of it. He just wanted to help his friends.

Fleas lived in a basement flat of a three-storey terraced house on a quiet residential street in Stamford Hill. He shared the flat with his girl Barbara, one of those British-born black girls who thought being with a Yardie was about as exciting as life got. She doted on Fleas, couldn't do enough for him, despite the fact that he regularly beat her and flaunted his other women in her face. The first time I saw her – she had come to see Fleas on the Front – I couldn't take my eyes off her. It was a hot summer's day and she had dressed accordingly in a yellow, figure hugging mini-dress with a plunging neckline. It didn't seem right to me that someone like Fleas, with his peanut head and matchstick frame, got to have regular sex with such a hot girl. He was no fool. He knew what a catch Barbara was and didn't take any chances with her, especially not with his boys. He was the alpha male among them, and they feared him, but Barbara had the type of body to make them forget their fears.

To abduct someone like Fleas required a bit of thought. Much too sure of themselves, Mitch was all for jumping him in broad daylight, but I wanted no part of what I saw as a very dumb move. For one thing, it wouldn't be easy to subdue Fleas and bundle him into Mitch's 3-series Bimmer without attracting witnesses, and for another, it was well known that Fleas never left home without his Beretta. Given that we were also armed

– the Browning was now back in my possession – there was just too strong a risk of gunplay. As I saw it, the better option was to gain access to Fleas's flat when he was out and surprise him on his return. And we wouldn't even have to break in. We simply had to watch the flat till we knew Barbara was home alone then knock on the door, take her hostage and wait. Mitch initially objected to my plan. It wasn't gangster enough for him, there was no action and no audience, but the moment I mentioned Barbara he did a complete U-turn.

Staking out Fleas's flat was not as straightforward as I had hoped. Mitch had to park his car far enough down the street to be out of sight, yet close enough to the flat to be able to observe the comings and goings. We managed it, but only just. Trying to see if any patterns emerged, we watched the flat for five nights in a row, from Monday through to Friday, working in shifts, starting at five in the afternoon and finishing at midnight. We didn't bother with the weekend because we were big ravers and not even Fleas could keep us from our weekly rendezvous with Sir Biggs Hi-Fi. Fortunately, our five-day surveillance gave us all the information we needed.

For a gangster, Fleas turned out to be quite the homebody. He came home every evening at eight or thereabouts. Herself no stranger to routine, Barbara usually came home from her job – she worked in a trendy clothes shop in Islington – around six. Our window of opportunity, then, was the two hours in between.

As the big day approached, I started to lose my nerve. To steady myself, I focussed on two things: I thought long and hard about how close my brother had come to dying and the fact that my parents had been forced to hide under their bed while Fleas and his crew had been spraying their flat with bullets. And even that wasn't enough to stiffen my resolve. Finally I had to resort to drugs. In the hours before we set out on our mission, we freebased half an ounce of Charlie. We also spent a lot of time demonising and dehumanising our enemy in order to make the job of killing him that much easier. Working ourselves into a vein-popping, eye-bulging state of rage, we agreed that Fleas was a cockroach who deserved to be squashed. Barbara's character was also assassinated. For allowing a piece of shit like Fleas put his cock inside her she was nothing but a filthy whore. There was no question that she too would have to be snuffed out, but only after we'd had our way with her and made Fleas watch the show. It hardly seemed credible to me that I should have found myself in that situation, plotting such vile crimes with all the deliberateness and calculation of a sociopath, but that was the person I had become. How it happened I neither knew nor, by that stage, cared.

Fleas hadn't trained his woman very well. Either that or he didn't think I'd come after him at home. Anyhow, when we knocked on his door Barbara opened it without checking. It was all over in seconds. Immediately she appeared in the doorway, Benjy clamped his paw over her mouth and shoved her back into the flat. We were in. Quick and easy, no noise and no witnesses. The first part of the task had been accomplished.

In the front room, we gagged Barbara, tied her hands and feet and lay her on the floor facing the wall. Mitch and Benjy then went off to search the rest of the flat, hoping to find some kind of booty lying around, leaving me to watch Barbara. She was wearing an outsize yellow T-shirt and a pair of skin-tight black leggings that showed off her perfect arse. Seeing in her that position gave me an immediate hard-on and I was tempted to take her right there and then. For several minutes I stood picturing the scene: her lying flat on her stomach and me fucking her hard from behind. With all the Charlie I had in me, my heart was pumping at the thought, but I was determined not to touch her till Fleas got back. I needed him there to bear witness.

My thoughts were interrupted when I noticed that Barbara was trying to turn around. I gave her a quick dig in the ribs with my heel and she groaned and resumed her original position. The spell now broken, I turned away and began scanning the front room. Apart from a red two-piece sofa, a small dining table with two mismatched chairs and a mini Hi-Fi system, there was nothing in it. No pictures on the white walls, no ornaments on the mantelpiece over the bricked-up fireplace, no rugs or mats on the laminate floor, no plants. There wasn't even a TV. I couldn't work that one out. Even in the days when I was squatting we had a small black and white set. Maybe Fleas and Barbara were among that strange breed who didn't like watching telly, but whatever the reason for so glaring an omission I was surprised to be having such mundane thoughts at a time when I should have been pumped up and focussed on the job at hand.

As if to remind me to get my mind right, Mitch returned looking seriously pissed off to have found only a few bits of jewellery and forty quid in cash.

'What a couple of paupers,' he said and kissed his teeth.

Soon after that Benjy appeared, looking similarly disappointed. 'This yard is proper dry. Even the kitchen.'

I couldn't believe what I was hearing.

'The kitchen? The fuck you looking in there for?'

Benjy gave me a condescending smile.

'That's the first place you look. You know how many drums I've broken into and found money and shit hidden in the freezer?'

Mitch said, 'Stop lying. You know you was really looking for food.'

They had a little snigger at that and punched fists for emphasis. They were acting like a couple of naughty schoolboys. I needed them to focus.

Just then Barbara made a moaning noise. 'Shut the fuck up bitch!' said Mitch, before adding, 'Damn! I can't wait to stab her pussy.'

He then turned to me and said, 'We really gotta wait till that eediot Fleas gets back?'

'Yeah,' I replied. 'We do. That's the whole damn point. I want that battyboy sitting ringside when she gets it. So back the fuck up.'

In an effort to take control of the situation, I had deliberately put an edge on my voice. I didn't have to worry about Benjy, but it was crucial that Mitch understood that I was running the show and to make sure he knew it I brandished the gun for the first time since we arrived. It had the desired effect.

'Hold it down,' said Mitch.

'Yeah,' said Benjy, 'man was only ramping, for fuck's sake.'

I glowered at them. 'Yeah, well, I didn't come here to ramp.

This ain't some kinda game.'

They stood there watching me, not sure what to do or say next. Benjy didn't seem so much afraid as suspicious, as if he thought I might turn on him.

Mitch on the other hand smiled and said, 'Chill out, Si. We're all bredrens here, remember?'

I knew that tone, he only ever used it when he couldn't get the better of me by bullying means, but I wasn't playing with him that night. When he realised this, he went and sat on the sofa, where he was quickly joined by Benjy.

For several minutes none of us spoke. Occasionally, Mitch would cast a wary glance in my direction, checking on me. I stared him down, determined to make him understand that I was in the zone and that I meant business. Benjy seemed unsure what to do, who to side with. He kept looking from me to Mitch, smiling at both of us in turn, clearly not wanting to take sides. Aware of the tension between me and Mitch he was trying, as ever, to keep us from tearing each other apart. From the corner of my eye I saw Barbara crane her neck a little, trying to see what was going on behind her, but she was very careful not to move too much, like a bird that had been caught by three razor-clawed cats and was trying to play dead. The tension in the room began to mount. After a while I couldn't bear it anymore and went to the window to have a peep behind the curtain. The street was a dead as a desert.

With my anxiety levels about to go through the roof, I sucked in a couple of deep breaths and went and sat at the dining table. I remained there for the next half an hour or so, gun in hand,

163

waiting. In that time, Mitch, clearly determined not to agitate me further, stayed schtum. At one point he rolled himself a spliff and offered me a drag, as a kind of peace offering, but I refused and he passed it to Benjy instead. I needed something stronger, and so I got out my little packet of Charlie and had two quick snorts, sniffing the powder from the back of my hand before licking the empty packet clean and then wiping it against my teeth and gums. It was good stuff, hadn't been cut to nothing with Ajax or washing up powder. The rush it gave me was indescribable. I felt as if I was inflating, every part of my body seemed to expand. Then my ears started humming, I started getting palpitations and my mouth filled with saliva. I was conscious of where I was and what I was doing, but at the same time I had the sense of not being present, a feeling of being separated from my surroundings. Panic and paranoia then set in. I looked at Mitch and was convinced that he and Benjy were plotting to jump me. Struggling to keep it together, I gripped the gun and for the next while kept looking at my watch. I was getting impatient for the thing to be over. Seeing Barbara on the floor like that, like an animal waiting to be slaughtered, sickened me. What the hell was I doing? She didn't deserve to be terrorised. Why didn't I put an end to her nightmare? Why not let the poor girl alone? My beef was with Fleas, why drag his girl into it?

When it reached eight o'clock I was practically climbing the walls. When it got to nine and Fleas still hadn't showed up I snapped. 'Fuck this for a laugh.' I marched across the room to Barbara and grabbed her under her armpits and dragged her back to the dining table and put her to sit on one of the

164

chairs. Mitch and Benjy unglued themselves from the sofa and came and joined me. With the three of us standing over her, Barbara lost it.

With a crazed look in her tear-filled eyes, she started shaking her head and moaning through her gag, her expression that of someone who believed her time had come and was making one last desperate plea to be spared. I said, 'Now listen carefully, Barbara. I'm gonna take off that gag, but I swear to God, if you even think about screaming…' I put the gun to her temple and she became so frightened her eyes virtually popped out of their sockets. '…That's right. Now, then. I want some answers.'

Benjy looked puzzled. He turned to Mitch as if in search of an answer to what I was doing but Mitch had his eyes fixed on Barbara, was running them all over her body. I said, 'You expecting your boyfriend back tonight?' She started making muted sounds, trying to speak through the gag. I passed the gun in front of her eyes. 'Remember. No screaming.' She nodded and I took off the gag.

As soon as it was out of her mouth she let out a shrill, ear-splitting scream. Mitch and Benjy immediately pounced on her and had the gag back in her mouth in a matter of seconds. They then stood back, waiting to see what I would do, waiting for instructions. I pondered my next move. I had to make Barbara talk. I had to know if she expected Fleas back that night and if so, roughly when. Looking at Mitch, it seemed pretty clear to me what he had in mind and so I decided to use him to scare Barbara into spilling the beans.

I turned to him and said, 'She's all yours.'

The words had barely left my lips before he was tearing at

her clothes. For a moment or two Benjy didn't move, he didn't seem to know what to do, and then he suddenly sprang into action and started helping Mitch. Virtually mad with fear, Barbara was now struggling and trying to scream through the gag, but of course it was useless and within minutes Mitch and Benjy had stripped her naked, exposing her full heavy breasts and thick black bush. When they started to get undressed themselves I brought a halt to the proceedings. 'Hold up a minute.' They froze, looked at me. Benjy had stripped down to his waist, whilst Mitch, determined to get in there first, had managed to shed everything barring his socks. I couldn't help but notice his small cock. 'Damn!' he said. 'What now, Si?' Barbara had stopped struggling and was now whimpering, looking between us with an expression that was one-part confusion to nine-parts terror. I said to her, 'I'm gonna ask you again. You expecting Fleas back tonight or what?' She stared at me, as if waiting for me to remove the gag, but I wasn't playing that game anymore. 'Just nod or shake your head.'

She waited a second or two, then nodded. 'OK. That's good. Now I need you to give me a rough time. I'm gonna count down from ten o'clock. When I get to the right time I want you to nod. You got that?' She stared at me for a few seconds, then nodded.

'Very good. Ten o'clock?'

She shook her head.

'Eleven?'

Another shake of the head.

'Midnight?'

She waited a moment, as though unsure of what she was

166

doing, then nodded quickly.

To make certain I had it right, I said, 'You're expecting him back around midnight?'

She nodded again, twice this time. She had to be telling the truth. It would explain why Fleas hadn't come home already. In which case the game was up. I wasn't going to sit around for another three hours. I was just too wired. The wait would have done my head in. The plan had gone wrong and it was now just a question of seeing what could be salvaged from the wreckage. Fleas would have to be taken down some other time. But until then I decided to send him a clear message.

I turned to Mitch and said, 'Do your t'ing.'

Within seconds he had Barbara lying on the floor, on her back. To penetrate her properly, he had to get Benjy to hold her down while he undid the bound around her ankles, at which point she began to kick and wriggle like a thing possessed. For all their superior strength, Mitch and Benjy just couldn't restrain her. Mitch, who was the stronger and more savage of the pair, smashed his fist into her face. After that Barbara didn't move again or make another sound. She hadn't been knocked out, she was still clearly conscious, but the fight had completely left her. From then on she lay as still as a corpse, her face swelling up almost by the second, while Mitch and Benjy, operating like some kind of wrestling tag team, took turns with her.

I stood watching them, almost in a state of shock at what I was seeing, at what I had orchestrated. I was utterly revolted. I hated myself for what I had done and for a moment, a brief moment, I thought about putting the gun to my head and pulling the trigger. But of course that would have required an act of courage. I continued to watch Mitch and Benjy, who were now in another place. They were acting like wild starving dogs mauling their kill.

Meanwhile, Barbara had scrunched her face up so tightly she had puppy wrinkles on her nose and crows' feet at the corners of her eyes. I didn't know why, but at the sight of that something came over me, some last vestige of compassion I guess, and I shouted, 'For fuck's sake, you two. That's enough!'

They completely ignored me. I may as well have been talking to myself. I got so angry that I moved in and clubbed Mitch round the head with the butt of the gun, sending him sprawling across the room, and then, before he could react, I put the gun to Benjy's forehead and said, 'You fucking deaf or what? I said enough!'

While Mitch sat rubbing his head, Benjy, who had frozen at the point of mounting Barbara, was propping himself up on his arms as if he was about to do press-ups.

'Take it easy with that fucking thing, Si. I hear you OK? I need to stand up. I'm getting cramp in my arms.'

I allowed him to stand up then ordered him to go sit next to Mitch. He did as he was told, pouting. Once I had the two of them sitting side by side in the nude, I looked at Barbara. By now she had backed herself into a corner and was sitting with her arms covering her breasts and her knees drawn up. Her face was as swollen as a puffer fish. With her wrists still bound and fat tears streaming down her bloated cheeks, she look bewildered, pitiful and as wretched as a war orphan. I moved towards her but at my approach she recoiled and started to whine, which stopped me dead in my tracks.

'What the fuck you waiting for?' said Mitch. 'Get on with it.'

I turned towards him and Benjy.

'Well?' said Mitch, 'you gonna out her or what? That's what we agreed, remember. No fucking witnesses.'

I said, 'She ain't stupid. She won't talk.' I looked at Barbara and said, 'Will you?'

For the first time that night she held my gaze, properly held it. Something, I don't know what, passed between us. I knelt down in front of her. She was about to start struggling but I said, 'Shhh....'

I slid the gag down to her chin. I didn't want to hurt her but I was also intensely aroused by her, not by the sight of her naked body, but by her vulnerability, by the helpless look in her eyes. I couldn't help myself and kissed her full on the mouth. She never took her eyes off me but I couldn't hold her stare and kept looking away.

'Will you?' I asked again.

She shook her head.

Mitch went crazy. He called Barbara a lying bitch and accused me of being a weak heart and insisted that if Barbara wasn't killed then the three of us were done for. He and Benjy were in a hurry now, hauling on their clothes with the speed of people who'd been caught asleep while war raged all around them. Mitch had been right, I knew that Barbara would run to the police the first chance she got but I just didn't care anymore, about any of it. I was worn out, drained, I wanted the nightmare to end.

I stood up and was suddenly seized by a desperate desire to leave the flat. I needed to be outside, I needed to breathe air that didn't reek of sex and cheesy feet and evil, and so, in the middle of their rant, I trained the gun on Mitch ordered him

169

to leave. For the first time that night he defied me.

'What the fuck you talking about? We ain't going nowhere.'

By now he and Benjy were fully dressed, looked almost like human beings again.

Benjy said, 'So what's it gonna be, Si?'

Mitch drew his blade.

We stood facing each other, a few metres apart, like gunfighters at the ready.

I wasn't backing down.

The only way they would harm Barbara any further was over my dead body.

'I'm warning you two, don't test me. I mean it, you bes' splurt before I put it on you proper.'

Mitch said, 'You ain't got the fucking balls Simon and you know it.'

I pointed the gun at him. 'I don't think Django would agree with you.'

That wiped the smirk off his face.

Benjy said, 'Come Mitch, let's blow this gaff.'

Mitch continued to stare at me.

Benjy had to tug his sleeve to get his attention. 'Come on, man. Let's dus'. We're done here.'

He started pulling Mitch towards the door, the two of them moving backwards, keeping a wary eye on me the whole time. When they reached the door, Mitch said, 'You're a fucking fool, Simon,' before he and Benjy turned and left.

Shortly afterwards I heard the front door slam. I went to the window to make sure they had actually gone. I got there just in time to catch a glimpse of them before they disappeared from view. At that point I heard the front door slam again and moments later I saw Barbara dash from the house, still gagged and bound at the wrists, still naked. Before she made her escape proper, she had the presence of mind to check which way Mitch and Benjy had gone. Once she had spotted them in the distance she sprinted off in the opposite direction, her heavy breasts undulating, like a streaker in the dark.

That night I wandered the streets for hours, like a vagrant, drunk with guilt and remorse. Eventually, around two in the morning, exhaustion overcame me and I took a cab to Finsbury Park, where I checked into a hotel for the night. It was a desperate measure. In those days the hotels and B&B's in Finsbury Park were the worst kind of fleapit knocking shops, but I couldn't risk going back to the flat share and there was no way I was going to my parents'. My body may have been worn out from all the walking but my mind was still fully awake. I lay on top of the bedcovers – they were just too stiff and old and full of I didn't know what to actually get under them – and reflected on the night's sickening events. Even at that early stage, as a way of dealing with the shame, I began to rationalise and make excuses. I was out of my mind on drugs. I had been seriously provoked. Mitch and Benjy were the animals, not me. I may have led them to the water, but I had no power to make them drink. And when all was said and done, had I not come to Barbara's rescue? The fact that she was still alive was down to me. That had to count in my favour. Surely that meant I was not a monster. But it was no use. The more I tried to ease my guilt the more it weighed on me, the more it threatened to crush me. By the time the dawn light started to penetrate my cramped cell – no easy task with the amount of grime on the windows – I was so full of disgust and self-hatred I could barely breathe.

The fact that I turned myself in did not help me in court. My brief used it in his plea for leniency but it didn't work. The judge gave me ten years. After he had passed sentence on me, one of Barbara's family, a woman, shouted from the gallery, 'You shoulda got life you evil sonofabitch!'

My parents were nowhere to be seen. Too ashamed, they just couldn't bring themselves to attend court. Only Theodore turned up, accompanied by several of his suited church brothers. Before I was taken down, the judge gave me permission to read out a statement I had prepared earlier. It was a carefully worded apology to Barbara, but no sooner had I opened my mouth than members of her family started booing in an attempt to drown me out. The judge had to order them to be quiet or face being charged with contempt of court. After I'd finished my statement and was about to be led from the dock, I turned to Theodore. He waved and mouthed something but I couldn't read his lips properly. Later, as I sat in the court holding cells waiting to be taken to prison, one of the escorting officers said to me, 'I wouldn't worry too much. With good behaviour you'll be out in about seven.' I thought he was being sympathetic, but then he quickly added, 'More's the pity.' Not long after that I was put in a van along with a few other convicts and driven away to start my sentence.

It took the police several more months to track down first Benjy, who was picked up in Tottenham, and then Mitch, who had been hiding out at his cousin's in Elephant and Castle. They didn't contest the rape charge, but tried to argue that I had forced them into it at gunpoint, contradicting everything that Barbara had told the police in her statement. For some reason the judge chose to believe Barbara. For their temerity in trying to deceive the court, Mitch and Benjy got twelve years apiece with a recommendation that they serve a minimum of ten.

* * *

Tortured by guilt and remorse, I twice tried to commit suicide in prison, slashing my wrists both times. The first time I had to be taken to an outside hospital, the bleeding was that bad, but the second attempt was not as serious, more a cry for help, and I was bandaged up and given counselling. I talked a lot in those sessions, the counsellor sitting on a chair next to my bunk, but the words sounded empty. I couldn't see a way back from where I was. How would I ever be able to walk upright again after what I'd done? What could I possibly do to redeem myself in the eyes of society? It seemed clear to me that I was destined to see out the rest of my days as a social outcast, skulking about the fringes of society, my head cast forever downwards. It was at this point that Theodore decided to take me in hand. Whenever he came to see me, he'd make me close my eyes and bow my head while he asked God to forgive me. He also told me that I had to find a way to forgive myself, saying that it was the only way I'd be able to go on and live a normal life again.

During the dark days of my imprisonment and immediately after my release his words proved to be a great comfort. Even so, I didn't believe them to be entirely true. If we do wrong and are genuinely remorseful, it's not enough that we forgive ourselves, we have to know that we've also been forgiven. The circle has to be complete, but I feared that would never be the case for me. On Theodore's advice, I tried to contact Barbara, I wrote to her from prison expressing my deepest shame and regret and begging her forgiveness. It took her months to reply and when she did, she was blunt: 'I hope you rot in hell for what you did. Never contact me again.' So there it was. I didn't like to think it, but maybe there really were some things in life that were unforgivable.

* * *

I served my time on E-Wing, unofficially known as Fraggle Rock as it housed all the rapists and child molesters. It was twenty-three-hour bang-up, with an hour of exercise, away from the main prison population. We had to be separated for our own safety. I did everything in my cell. Sometimes I had it to myself, sometimes I had to share. I preferred those times when I was alone. Time dragged like I never thought possible. I looked forward to my visits like a plant needing rain. After saying they couldn't face seeing me locked up, my parents relented and visited me at least once a month. They never had much to say beyond enquiring into my well-being. Mum always thought I looked skinny and said I should eat more and she always brought food with her. I was glad for it as the prison food was disgusting. Dad mostly sat in silence, occasionally asking if I was behaving myself and warning me not to do anything that would cause me to miss my release date.

'There is a great deal of difference between seven years and ten.'

He'd always been one for stating the obvious.

Theodore's visits were the worst. With him it was God this and Jesus that, all the time. He was now playing for his church team and coaching some kids in the area who had got into trouble with the law. He was really proud of the work and said he wanted me to get involved when I was released. I was tempted, I had to do something when I got out, but I was wary of Theodore's motives: he was always trying to convert me to what he called 'Christ's army.'

* * *

The main activity in prison was bodybuilding. Inmates on Fraggle Rock were not allowed to use the gym and had to their sit-ups, pull ups and press ups in their cell. Most of the guys I shared with were obsessed with expanding their muscles, whereas I was more interested in expanding my mind. In prison I took to reading in a big way. I usually had at least a dozen books in my cell at any given point, a mixture of titles borrowed from the prison library and ones my family brought in on visits. Without really meaning to, I noticed that my reading habits changed significantly during my time in prison. At first I ate up all the crime fiction, particularly of the hard-boiled American school, but eventually I grew tired of reading predictable stories that glamourised killing and violence and decided to broaden my tastes. I sampled a bit of sci-fi, which was all the rage in prison but which didn't appeal to me at all, and for a time I ploughed through quite a number of the so-called classics in an effort to plug the gaps in my reading, none of which I found particularly enjoyable. The language was too old-fashioned and I couldn't connect to the people or the world. And then I started reading prison memoirs. Here, at last, were stories I could relate to, written by people from very similar backgrounds as me. *The Autobiography of Malcom X* kept me absorbed for days while I was reading it and stayed with me long after I'd finished it. I was especially affected by the passage describing his conversion to Islam while serving his latest prison term. It has to be one of the most powerful accounts of a journey from blindness to sight that's ever been written. Reading it gave me hope, made me think that I could still make something of myself, that it was not too late for me to turn things around.

As well as reading for pleasure, I did a lot of academic reading in prison. Leaving school without any qualifications had been gnawing away at my conscience for years, like unfinished business, and I seized my opportunity through the prison's distance-learning programme to take my GCEs and A-levels. All were gained with high marks, yet I felt unsatisfied with what I'd accomplished. I was proud of my success, for sure, but it didn't feel authentic.

When I first got to prison it hadn't been possible to avoid Mitch and Benjy, though I'd wanted to. We spent a year together on the same wing. Our interactions were always tense. Incredibly, Mitch was still carrying a grievance and we actually had a fight one day in the exercise yard. Benjy had to separate us. From then on I tried to stay out of their way and was relieved when eventually they got transferred; first Benjy, who ended up somewhere near Manchester, and then Mitch, who got sent to a place in Maidstone. I knew that at some point I'd be transferred as well – it was rare for long-term inmates to serve their sentence in one prison – and I was praying not to be sent to the same place as either of them. It never happened. In fact, I never saw them again.

* * *

Little by little, as my release date drew nearer, I began to imagine what sort of life I wanted for myself and, more importantly, where I wanted to live. Instinctively I knew I didn't want to return to London. I certainly didn't want to return to Hackney. A clean break was the best option. I knew that. I also knew it wouldn't be easy for me to start a new life anywhere else. Hackney was my home. It was all I had ever known. I was tied to the place. I had too much to lose by leaving, the most important thing being my family. Despite the heartache I had caused them, they had stood by me. Without their loyalty and support I doubt I would have made it through the seven long years I spent inside. Their value to me had never been higher and I had no desire to see it depreciate ever again.

I was let out of prison in the autumn of 1993. For a long time after I returned, I barely left the house. The shame of seeing people who knew about my crime was crippling. I had moved in with my parents on the understanding that it was a

177

temporary arrangement until I was on my feet again but ended up spending over a year with them. I wasn't happy to be living under their roof at the age of twenty-four, but circumstances, not least of a financial kind, dictated my actions. I hated my life at that point. Discounting the fortnightly visits to my probation officer and my attempts to find work, I did little but sit at home and brood. Very occasionally, if I was feeling adventurous or if the folks were getting on my nerves, I'd go and watch a movie at an out-of-the-way cinema, taking back streets and doing everything possible to avoid being seen. On even rarer occasions, when I could be bothered to go to the stadium and queue up for tickets, I'd go and watch Spurs play at the weekend. Most of the time I'd go alone, but occasionally, if he could make it, if he didn't have church commitments, Theodore would come with me.

I knew I had to find a job, any job, and fast. My parents were not in a position to support me and I wouldn't have allowed them to anyway. Unfortunately, finding a job was easier decided than achieved. As I began the process, it became immediately and depressingly clear that I was unemployable. My CV was almost a total blank. Apart from the few months I'd spent at Wimpy immediately after leaving school, I'd never had a proper job in my life. With no experience of the work place and no marketable skills, I was struggling to get even a menial position.

My criminal record didn't help.

As for my cherished GCEs and A-Levels, they were next to worthless. I had left school to become a work-shy dole-scrounger and those chickens had now come home to roost.

I used to be contemptuous of wage slaves, but after leaving prison I came to see them in an altogether more respectful light. To hold down a job, particularly if you're only doing it for the money, is no mean feat. There's much to admire in people who are prepared to make that kind of investment in their future, people who are able to take the long view. One of my best friends at school had gone on to become a nine-to-fiver, and whenever I used to see him on his way back from his shift – I was never up early enough to catch him on his way *to* it – I couldn't help but laugh. Dressed in his regulation donkey jacket – he worked for Hackney Council as a parks attendant – I thought he looked daft. He hadn't crossed my mind in years, but during that period when I was tramping around looking for work, he was all I could think about. Wherever he was, I felt sure that he was not only gainfully employed, but that he also had a mortgage and savings and a car and could maybe afford to take a holiday now and then; while I, the cool drop-out and now ex-con, couldn't even get a job collecting rubbish.

With my job hunt proving fruitless, I panicked and started applying for any and everything. For a dispiriting period of about six months I couldn't even get a response to my letters, never mind interviews. Finally, on the advice of my probation officer, I turned to a handful of temping agencies that specialised in the sort of work for which I was suitable – anything physical that required neither experience nor formal qualifications – but even they were reluctant to take me on. All the same, I managed to blag my way onto the books of a couple of the leading agencies, having sworn to them that I was prepared to take anything, anywhere, at a moment's notice. I must have impressed them, since it wasn't long before the job offers started coming in. I turned down nothing, no matter how demeaning or low-paid. The idea was to convince the agencies of my reliability and willingness to work in the hope that the jobs would keep coming in. It didn't quite pan out that way. There were too many dry spells followed by too few days of rain. I couldn't establish any kind of rhythm, but somehow I got by.

The work was depressing. It reminded me of a book I had read in prison, *My Golden Trades* by Ivan Klima. The author had described the type of work he had to do whilst trying to become a writer. Most of the jobs were menial and laborious, but Klima invests them with, if not nobility, then at least respectability. The jobs I endured could not be rescued by poetry. Warehouse-filling, hod-carrying, shelf-stacking, dish-washing, office-cleaning, night-portering, road sweeping, dog-walking, leafleting, canvassing, envelope-stuffing. Here were jobs to kill the soul, and I did them with about as much enthusiasm as a galley slave. This kind of work did not acquaint me with the dignity of simple toil. Nor did it make me appreciate the thankless but essential contribution being made to society by the ordinary workingman. What it did was throw my low position in society into sharp, demoralising relief. There was no point trying to dress it up. I was down there amongst the dregs, working alongside people who had no alternatives, no choices, people who were barely surviving, despite the fact that they regularly put in fifty- to sixty-hour shifts a week. On average, I only worked with these people for a few days at a stretch, coming in at the start of the week and often gone by the middle of it, but during these short

180

periods it was all I could do not to become infected by the anger, bitterness and self-loathing of my workmates.

I continued to do a variety of dead end jobs until, at last, I found something that paid quite well and didn't make me want to kill myself: doing deliveries by van. The work took me all over London and the south east and sometimes as far as the midlands, delivering everything from coat hangers to rolls of bubble wrap. I loved the freedom of it, the sense of being alone on the road. I even liked those moments when I was stuck in traffic, which happened a lot, especially in London. I'd use the time to listen to the radio, mostly news and current affairs programmes. Being in prison for seven years, I felt totally out of the loop and had a lot of catching up to do. I did that job, off and on, for six years, making runs to some of England's most down-at-heel towns; white, predominantly working class towns where people loved the Royal Family, ate fish and chips several times a week and put a Union Jack in their windows all year round and not just when the England football team was playing in major tournaments; towns like Duddenham.

Epilogue

I left Len's and dashed home, my heart pounding. As soon as I got in I unplugged my landline, switched off my mobile, closed all the curtains and double-locked the front door. Then, needing something comforting, I went into the kitchen and made myself a hot chocolate. Leaning against the counter with the mug in my hands I became so distracted that it went cold. Try as I did, I just couldn't shake the images of the rape from my mind. It was the only thing I could think about, as if it had happened that day and not twenty years previously. The memory had been getting clearer by the day, the pieces of the mental jigsaw slotting themselves neatly into place, and now the full picture had been assembled. It felt like I was watching some sick slasher movie that I couldn't switch off. By contrast, I never thought once about the bombing. In fact, I couldn't remember when I had last thought about it. The transfer, it seemed, was now complete.

When I could no longer bear my thoughts I decided to call Theodore. At that moment he was the only person I wanted to speak to. I chose to call him with my mobile, and when I

183

switched it on I noticed I had several missed calls from numbers I didn't recognise. Most of the callers had tried once and given up, but a few had been more persistent and had called several times. These I took to be journalists looking for a quote. I'd also had calls from Theodore, Dave, Rhona and Richard but only Theodore, Richard and Rhona had left messages. Theodore said that he would be praying for me and that I should call him as soon as possible, Richard had left a long rambling message to say that, in light of the revelations, my stock was at an all-time high and that I should call him if I was interested in making 'some serious money', while Rhona had called to say that one of her patients had just come into the surgery and shown her the article and that we really needed to talk. Before she hung up she asked me to come and see her after she'd finished work. I didn't like the sound of her voice one bit. It was too sombre, too resigned. It was the voice of someone who needed to make a tough decision and was well on the way to making it. I thought about calling her right away. If she wanted nothing further to do with me, I figured I should know sooner rather than later, but I didn't call her because if she was going to dump me I wanted her to do it when she wasn't distracted by thoughts of fillings and root canals.

I called Theodore on his mobile. He was at work, but he managed to take a few minutes to talk to me. When I told him that I hadn't left the house since the story broke, that I didn't dare go out for the shame, he said, 'Let him who is without sin cast the first stone. Don't worry about what other people are thinking, bruv. Try and go about your life as normal. Ignore the papers. Don't read 'em. Remember, today's news, tomorrow's chip wrapper. It'll soon blow over. And if it all gets

184

too much, then now might be the time for you to go and see the folks. You could even take Rhona. I'm sure she'd love it.' It was typical of him to consider Rhona. He didn't regard what she and I had as that serious, but it was a mark of his respect for me that he never tried to deny her existence.

'I dunno about that. I have a sneaky feeling that me and her are done as of today.'

He went silent for a moment then said, 'Why? Because of the story?'

'I think so. I'll know for sure when I go and see her this evening, but she left a message on the phone and she doesn't sound too happy. I wouldn't be surprised if she wants out.'

Theodore sighed. 'That'd be a shame. I hope it doesn't happen, but if it does, then I pray you'll see sense and come back to London. After all, what reason would you have for staying in that place if you and Rhona broke up?'

He didn't need to ask the question, and I know he wasn't really looking for an answer, but still I said, 'None.'

The hours rolled by, slowly. Locked up in the flat, I felt more like a prisoner than when I was actually incarcerated. With a few hours left to kill before Rhona got home, I gave in to the temptation to check out the TV news. I had to see if my story had been picked up. Ten minutes of flicking between the channels showed that it hadn't. There was still a chance it would appear later that day or in the days to come, but I doubted it. The news stations had so far ignored my fame, which had been an invention of the tabloid press, and whilst I didn't want to tempt fate, it seemed they would also ignore my disgrace.

I had only myself to blame. I should never have spoken to the press. In the wake of the bombing, all my instincts had told me to steer clear of publicity, to keep my head down, but ultimately the pull had proved just too strong. The day I called him to get advice about whether I should sell my story, the first thing Theodore had said was, 'It's up to you. But I have to say that all the money in the world won't solve your problems. It won't make you feel any better about yourself. If anything, it'll probably make you feel worse.' How true. I had almost a hundred grand tucked away in the bank, earning interest, but it was about as comforting to me as a last meal is to a condemned man. I didn't want any of it. I decided that I would honour my promises to give a bit to Rhona, Sky and my parents, then donate the rest to charity.

Just as it had been the first time around, there were innocent people in my life who would have to share in my shame. Rhona would have to hide her face, whilst Sky was probably even then being teased by her schoolmates. There was no escape for them. Just as there'd been no escape for Theodore and my parents during the original scandal. At least my parents were now in Jamaica and would be spared further humiliation, but Theodore would have to go through it all over again. For all his bravado, for all his claims that his faith insulated him from the judgements of others, the truth is he had suffered and would suffer again the stigma of being the brother of a convicted rapist.

It was well after dark before I plucked up the courage to go and see Rhona. I had waited because I wanted the activity on our street to die down before venturing outside. The walk from my place to Rhona's took no more than ten minutes door to door, but to avoid even the slightest chance of running into someone I decided to drive. I sneaked out of the house and walked briskly across the road to where my car was parked. I was about to put the key in the door when I sensed a presence behind me. I swivelled in an instant and came face to face with Trevor. He had two of his friends with him. I didn't recognise them. To make sure I didn't try to run, they flanked me. Trevor eyeballed me for what seemed an age.

Eventually I said, 'Well, you gonna stand there all night holding your dick or you and your girls gonna actually do something?'

He smiled, which was the signal for his boys to start inching towards me. He himself actually took a step backwards, giving his mates room to work. At that point I relaxed. If I had any fight in me I couldn't summon it. I couldn't be bothered. When Trevor's henchman pounced on me I put up a token resistance. In no time they had me in an arm and neck lock. Only then did Trevor step forward. 'I'm gonna show you what we do to rapists round here.'

They left me in a crumpled heap at the front wheel of my car. My face, which had taken most of the punishment, I couldn't feel. I had suffered some kind of internal damage as well, possibly a broken rib or two. When I tried to stand up the pain in my side made me cry out and slump back to the ground. For a moment I thought about crawling across the street to my flat but the pain was just too severe to move. In the end I took out my mobile and called Dave. He answered on the first ring. Through my swollen bloody lips I just about managed to say, 'Dave. Need your help.' I didn't have the energy to say anything else. No longer able to keep myself upright, I toppled sideways and the phone fell from my hand onto the pavement. For the next minute or so I could hear Dave saying, 'Hello. Hello. Simon? You there?' Soon afterwards I passed out.

I woke up in hospital. Dave had driven round to mine and found me lying on the pavement. Later he joked that he had almost given himself a hernia trying to put me in his car. I spent the night in hospital. Before being discharged, one of the patients stopped me as I was leaving the ward and asked for my autograph. Dave, who had come to pick me up, was practically shoved aside. I couldn't believe it. There I was, my face full of stitches, my ribs bound as tightly as a mummy, walking on crutches, being asked for an autograph. The patient, a gaunt, forty-something woman dressed in a hospital-issue gown and slippers, wasn't even interested to know what had happened to me. My celebrity was all that concerned her. She clearly didn't know about the revelations and I wondered how long it would be before she found out and ripped up the piece of paper on which I had scribbled, 'To Jenny. Lots of love, Simon Weekes.'

Dave put me up in his flat and took three days off work especially to take care of me. In that time he waited on me hand and foot, without complaint and without expectation of reward. I offered him some money, not for services rendered, but just because I had more than I needed and he didn't seem to have enough and it felt like the right thing to do. He refused, was almost insulted. When I told him that I wanted to do something for him, that I needed to, he said, 'You're a mate. That's enough.'

Whilst I was convalescing at Dave's, I thought about calling Theodore to tell him what had happened, but I didn't want him to fret unnecessarily so I decided to leave it till I was back on my feet. I also called Rhona, several times, but she never picked up. I left messages but she never got back to me. In desperation I called Sky on her mobile. As soon as she answered I could hear the tension in her voice. When I asked after Rhona, she said, 'She's here.'

She was whispering to avoid being overheard by her mum, but it didn't work because I heard Rhona say, 'Is that Simon?'

Sky said to me, 'see you soon,' and moments later Rhona came on the line.

'That was a cheap trick calling Sky like that.'

She was right.

'Look,' she said, 'I haven't been taking your calls because I just needed a bit of time to sort my feelings. I probably didn't handle it right and I'm sorry about that, I'm sorry I wasn't there for you. I panicked, that's all.' I heard her shuffling, probably getting more comfortable. I pictured her sitting down.

'Thing is, Simon, it's not only about you and me, there's Sky, too. I have to do what I can to protect her from all this.'

'Sky doesn't need protecting. She's a big girl.'

That hit a nerve. 'How the hell do you know what she needs from what she doesn't? When you have kids of your own then come back and talk to me.'

189

She paused, composed herself. 'I don't want to argue with you, Simon. Honestly, that's not what I want.'

'What do you want?'

She went quiet for a moment then said, 'I don't want to lose you.'

'You don't have to.'

'I know but it's hard, it's hard to figure out how to handle things at the moment. I can deal with the attention, but as I say, it's not fair on Sky. We've already had journalists calling up asking to speak to her.'

'What could they possibly want with her?'

'They wanted her to talk about you, they....' she hesitated, then went on, 'they were trying to get her to dig the dirt on you. I answered the phone so they never had the chance to speak to her directly. When I realised what they were after, I gave it to them straight: I told them you had never been anything but kind and loving to Sky and that she saw you almost as a father. Of course they didn't want to hear that and put the phone down on me.'

I was seething. The bastards. The very idea that I would hurt Sky....

It was time for plain speaking. I said, 'Be honest, do you want to keep this going or what?'

She didn't answer straight away, which made me panic.

Eventually she said, 'Yes. Yes I do, but....'

I could hear the fear in her voice, '...but maybe we should take a little break? Just a week or so until things die down? That sound reasonable to you?' It didn't sound reasonable at all but it did sound logical. 'Fair enough.'

Within a week I was feeling better, physically at any rate. I no longer needed the crutch and the bandages round my ribs had been removed. The summer was on its way out but it was still warm enough to sit outside.

One Sunday evening Dave and I went for a drink at our local and managed to find a seat in the busy beer garden at the back. I felt very nervous being out. I drew a lot of sideways glances and even a few whispered comments, but after two pints of Guinness I ceased caring. By the end Dave and I were laughing and joking and swapping amusing – and sometimes not so amusing – Blockbuster anecdotes, one of which featured Rhona. I had forgotten it but Dave, his speech slurred by all the lager he'd had, recounted it in full. We were at work one day when he asked me how old Rhona was. Without hesitation I said, 'Thirty-seven. Why?' Immediately he started laughing. When I asked him to share the joke, he pulled up Rhona's account on the computer screen and showed me her personal details, which included her date of birth. She was actually forty-one. I couldn't help myself and burst out laughing, at which point Dave said, 'That, my friend, is a clear case of mutton dressed as lamb.'

Later that afternoon, while Dave went off to get a round, I sent a text to Sky to say that I was going to spend a few days with my brother in London and to ask if she wanted me to bring her back something. She didn't want anything, but she said I should hurry back as she missed having me around. I thought that was the end of our little flurry of messages, but later, while Dave was suggesting that he and I spend a lads' weekend together in 'the smoke', I received another one from her. It read, '*u rlly do thse thngs 2 tht grl?*'

I hadn't expected that. It jolted me, like a punch to the stomach. I was tempted to ignore it, but Sky always had the ability to get what she wanted from me.

I sent her a reply saying, 'Yes I did, but it was a long time ago and I regret it very much.'

She didn't respond. I tried to imagine what she was thinking and hoped she wasn't judging me. A few moments later I felt my phone vibrate. '*hrd wot dad did. wot n arse. cll me frm lndn? hugs...xxx.*'

I blinked back the tears, hoping that Dave hadn't noticed.

At Kings Cross station I toyed with the idea of taking a taxi to Theodore's but the masochist in me opted for the tube. I convinced myself that it would be quicker and less hassle – I had arrived in London at the height of rush hour – but looking back I realised that I was simply testing myself. And it was indeed a test, but nowhere near as severe as the last time. 'Your brain has received a massive shock. It will recover in time.' That process, it seemed, was now in an advanced state.

Because he had to go to work, Theodore had left the key to his flat under the doormat. I let myself in, dumped my suitcase, called Rhona at the surgery to let her know I had arrived safely, then went out again. It was just too sunny and pleasant a day to be indoors. I went for a walk and ended up in a nearby park that was used mostly by mothers and toddlers. It had a paved play area, complete with swings and slides and a roundabout, and was screened from the busy road by a high wire-meshed fence. It was empty, except for a group of teenage boys having a kick-about. They were a mixed bunch ethnically, ranging in age from about twelve to fifteen. I sat on a weather-beaten bench and decided to watch them for a while. I was sitting only a few feet away but they barely noticed me. At that moment nothing was more important to them than the game. As I watched them, a memory from my childhood sprang unbidden into my mind. Theodore and I were playing 'Wembley' in the street immediately outside our house, jumpers for goal posts. Mum popped her head out the window and called us in. We completely ignored her and carried on playing. She was forced to come and get us, but when she tried to collar us, we ran rings round her, dribbled the ball between her legs, and tied her in knots. Despite herself, she ended up in fits of laughter. Dad came to the window to see what the commotion was then disappeared again. Moments later he too was in the street, and before long we were playing two against two: me and Mum versus Dad and Theodore. Several curtains twitched as we ran around making quite a noise. The game went on for some time, but I couldn't remember which team, if either, won.

Acknowledgements

I couldn't have written this novel without the love, encouragement and support of the following people: my ever-dependable friends James Wood, Kate Goldsworthy, Shenagh Cameron, Sabina Kubica and Nabil Elouahabi; my fellow Greeks Daphne Kauffmann, Spiros Arsenis, Daisy Arsenis, Lilla Dendrinou, Tommy Dendrinou, Kostis Karavias, John Harrison and Kathryn Harrison; my champion Rukhsana Yasmin; and last, but never surpassed, my big bro 'Yardie' and likkle sister Karen. I love you all.

An extra mention must go to Valerie Brandes for reminding me of what good editing is all about, and to Jazzmine Breary for encouraging me to keep an open mind about the things I make. You guys are an inspiration. Thanks for the faith you've shown in mon petit bouquin. Vive Jacaranda!